W9-AUN-462

Murphy's Island

Other books by
Colleen O'Shaughnessy McKenna:

Too Many Murphys
Fourth Grade Is a Jinx
Fifth Grade: Here Comes Trouble
Eenie, Meanie, Murphy, No!
Merry Christmas, Miss McConnell!

Murphy's Island

Colleen O'Shaughnessy McKenna

Scholastic Inc.
New York

Library of Congress Cataloging-in-Publication Data

McKenna, Colleen O'Shaughnessy.
Murphy's Island / Colleen O'Shaughnessy McKenna.
p. cm.
Summary: Collette Murphy has to go with her large, often trying family to a small island and start sixth grade there as the new girl in school.
ISBN 0-590-43552-3
[1. Islands—Fiction. 2. Moving, Household—Fiction. 3.Schools-Fiction. 4. Family life—Fiction.] I. Title.
PZ7.M478675Mu 1990
[Fic]—dc20 90-32172
CIP
AC

12 11 10 9 8 7 6 5 4 3 2 1 0 1 2 3 4 5/9
Printed in the U.S.A. 37
First Scholastic printing, November 1990

Murphy's Island

SP

Chapter One

"Collette, I can't believe your parents are doing this to you," said Marsha. "Sarah and I will have to start sixth grade by ourselves. It won't be the same at all!"

Collette yanked Marsha out of the way as Mr. Murphy swung another bike on top of the station wagon.

"Look at that car!" Marsha sputtered. "Collette, I don't think you're *ever* coming back. I thought your dad could only be a lawyer in Pittsburgh, anyway."

Collette shrugged, a little sad herself. A few weeks ago, she'd thought she'd be starting sixth grade at Sacred Heart with Marsha and Sarah, too. But then her father's case did not get settled out of court, and that meant he would have to be gone for nearly four months.

"We can all go," Mr. Murphy had announced one night, smiling as if they were going to Disney World. "We'll rent a place on Put-in-Bay Island and I'll take the ferry to Port Clinton every day. We can still be together."

Collette sighed, and plopped down on top of a milk crate. Of course, she wanted to be with her dad. Too bad that meant she couldn't be with her best friend, Sarah Messland.

"I sure am glad my dad isn't a lawyer," muttered Marsha. She crossed her arms and frowned at the car.

"We'll be right back after Christmas, Marsha. Maybe even before, if the case gets settled."

"Ha!" Marsha laughed, tossing back her head. "Your dad will probably mess up some weird island law and get the judge real mad. Then the jury will get mad and you'll be in seventh or eighth grade by the time you return."

Marsha paused as she looked down at Collette. "You'll probably marry someone from that dinky little island and spend the rest of your life cleaning fish."

"It's a beautiful island, Marsha," protested Collette. "I've sent you postcards for the past two summers . . ."

Marsha waved it all away with her hand. "Sure, sure . . . an island like that is OK for a two-week vacation, Collette. But *my* father told my mother last night that until your family went to Put-in — whatever . . . he had never even heard of it." Marsha sat down on the milk crate next to Collette. "And my father travels everywhere that's big enough to put on a map!"

"Oh Marsha, that's dumb," Collette said quickly. "Your dad doesn't know everything in the whole wide world, does he?"

Marsha raised one eyebrow, giving Collette a smug "yes-he-does" look.

"Oh who cares, anyway?" Collette's headache went up another notch. All morning Marsha had been bothering her and right now Collette's head was pounding from all the remarks she had stifled like, "Mind your own business" and "I won't miss your rude comments, Marsha."

Marsha and Collette were silent for a minute, watching Mr. and Mrs. Murphy carry suitcase after suitcase out to the car.

Part of Collette wished she could be left on the driveway. Then she could start school at Sacred

Heart Elementary, just as she had done for the past six years. Marsha's mother had even offered to let Collette stay with them for the next four months. The idea had horrified Mrs. Murphy because she thought families should stick together through thick and thin, in good times and in bad.

Collette sighed. She sure hoped that life on Put-in-Bay wouldn't be thin or bad.

"Tell your dad that the Battle of Lake Erie was fought off Put-in-Bay, Marsha. And my dad said Commodore Perry used Put-in-Bay as a harbor. . . ." Collette stopped and checked Marsha's face. Maybe the War of 1812 was important enough to impress Marsha. It was in history books and everything.

"All I know," Marsha began quietly, "is that your dad is kidnapping your whole family, just because *he* has to go sue somebody, and . . ."

"He is *not* kidnapping us, Marsha!" Collette stood up. Boy could Marsha pick the right words to say the wrong things.

Marsha stood and slowly brushed off her white shorts and yellow top. "Go ahead and enjoy your island, Collette. Sarah and I will be having a great time on our field trips to Heinz Hall watching *The*

Nutcracker and . . . and you and your brothers and little sister can go to the island and watch some old guy cleaning trout."

"Oh Marsha . . ." Collette knew that the next few months would be different. She was positive she would miss her best friend, Sarah. She would probably even miss Marsha. Marsha lived right across the street, and although they were not really friends, she was a part of Collette's everyday life. And Collette would miss her for that.

"Put-in-Bay has wineries, Perry Monument . . . lots of things to go see on a field trip, Marsha. Things Pittsburgh couldn't possibly have!"

Marsha opened her mouth, then clamped it shut fast when she didn't have anything smart-alecky to say back. She was silent for a second, thinking. As she chewed on the end of her ponytail, she started to smile. Jabbing Collette with her elbow, she began to snicker. "Good . . . good, Collette. I am really happy to know your dinky island has a winery available for field trips."

Collette studied Marsha's face, trying to see if she was kidding or serious.

"Yeah, Collette. Sounds real cultural to me. Sarah and I will be all dressed up, sitting in the balcony at the Benedum Center, listening to a symphony with the other sixth-graders, and you and your family will walk down to the winery and watch a bunch of peasants jump up and down in a barrel of grapes." Marsha started laughing hard at her own joke.

Collette swallowed quickly before the lump in her throat had time to grow any larger. Marsha's joke didn't bother her as much as the image of Sarah and Marsha sitting side by side in the balcony.

What if Marsha and Sarah became best friends while Collette was away? Four months was a long time. Time enough for most of the sixth grade to forget all about Collette Murphy. Besides, leaving a best friend alone for four months was a pretty dangerous thing.

Collette watched as her father came out with another load for the car. He jiggled each strap holding the bikes, standing at attention atop the car. Soon Collette and her family would be down the driveway and gone.

Four months was such a long time. Plenty of time for everything to change. Sixth grade at Sacred Heart would start without her, and maybe by Christmas vacation when she finally returned, no one would really even care. The hole she created when she left would already have closed tight.

Collette looked up at her old, red brick house. She felt so homesick already. She was so mixed up. The thought of her dad living in a hotel made her want to cry. But the thought of leaving Pittsburgh broke her heart.Why did lawyers have to leave town to earn a living anyway?

"Well, I better be going," Marsha said. She took a deep breath. "My mom said to be sure and drink bottled water the whole time you're away. Even though it's expensive and your mom will make a fuss."

"Why?"

Marsha raised both eyebrows. "Well, I'm sure an island as tiny as yours will not have a fancy water-treatment plant. They probably just run Lake Erie water through a giant coffee filter or something."

Collette stood up, red-faced. "You're nuts, Marsha. We've been on vacation there and we've never gotten sick."

"You've never drunk four months worth of

water, Collette. And my mom is sure you don't have *real* doctors on such a small island. Just . . . well, boat mechanics."

"Of course they have doctors, Marsha." Collette stood up straighter and tried to look calm. "It's probably a law that every island has to have a doctor."

Marsha blew her bangs up in the air and shrugged. It was Marsha's way of saying she didn't believe Collette at all.

Collette looked away. She was looking forward to an island adventure with her family. She *knew* the island was beautiful. But, the truth was, she was getting a little nervous about everything she didn't know about Put-in-Bay. What if Marsha's awful predictions turned out to be true?

"Time to go!" called Mrs. Murphy. She held open the screen door as Laura and Jeff ran out. "Stevie, come on. Kids, do you have to go to the bathroom?"

Laura raced over to Marsha and gave her a tight hug. "Bye, Marsha. I'll miss you. I'll miss you a whole lot!"

"Bye, Laura. I'll write you a letter as soon as you write me, OK?"

"OK, Marsha. Make sure no robbers get in our house. Most of my dolls are still inside waiting for me."

"Bye, Marsha!" Jeff called as he climbed into the backseat. He was nine and wouldn't hug anyone unless it was an aunt or grandmother.

"Well, I guess I'll see you in December," Collette said. She took a step closer to Marsha, but she didn't reach out and grab her for a good hug like she had with Sarah last night. She and Marsha really didn't have a hugging type of friendship.

"Here I come!" Stevie burst through the screen door with both hands outstretched. He came to a screeching halt in front of Marsha. He looked up at her, shoving his baseball cap back with a dirty fist. Blond curls exploded everywhere. "I bet you are really going to miss us, right, Marsha?"

Collette suddenly felt tears in her eyes as she saw Marsha's eyes get wet. Marsha bent down and hugged Stevie. He was only five and loved to hug everyone who paid attention to him. Collette knew Marsha only hugged her favorite people.

"I'll bring you a big fish back," Stevie called as he shoved Laura aside to climb into the backseat.

Collette and Marsha both watched as Mr. Murphy started the car and Mrs. Murphy handed the house key to Marsha. "Give this to your mom for us, OK, Marsha."

This was it.

"Well, bye," said Collette weakly. She felt hot, fat tears trying to spill out. She hadn't cried last night when she said good-bye to her truest, best friend, Sarah. But suddenly she felt like crying till she ran out of tears.

"Bye," said Marsha. She flung out both arms like lobster claws and hugged Collette tight.

"Write me," called Marsha as she ran down the driveway. "Bye Stevie, bye Jeff, bye Laura . . ." By the time Marsha had called out everyone's name, she was at the end of the driveway.

"Don't let anything fun happen till I get back," Collette shouted. "Make sure you and Sarah write to me . . . a lot!"

Marsha stood on the side porch and gave one last wave.

Collette raised her hand, homesick already. As nice as Put-in-Bay was, an island could never be home.

Chapter Two

"Why can't *I* ever be the guy to hold the ticket?" asked Stevie. It was the seventh time he had asked, and now even Mrs. Murphy was trying to ignore him.

"You just let the big guys hold things 'cause you like them better," continued Stevie. He tugged on his father's sleeve. "Can't I hold it for twenty-sixteen minutes? Then I'll give it back."

Collette groaned in the backseat. "Stevie, be quiet about the ticket. If you lost it, Daddy would have to pay the full fare on the turnpike. You wouldn't want that, would you?"

"Yeah," added Jeff. "Then we would have to sell you to get the money." Jeff snickered. "I bet we could get at least five cents for you."

Laura's eyes flew open. "Don't sell Stevie!"

Their mother twisted in her seat, running her fingers through her dark hair. "Of course we won't sell Stevie. Now stop the teasing, and Stevie, stop talking about the ticket. Hey honey, you can hold the map if you want."

"Not the map," Mr. Murphy said quickly. "Let him hold . . . hold that box of tissues if you want to hold something."

Collette and Jeff started laughing. Stevie started crying. Loudly. "Stop this car then, you mean guys. I'm going to run away and live with nice guys who will let me hold good stuff. Even gold!"

Mrs. Murphy started to sigh, then looked out the window. Collette knew her mother was tired from packing, calling the electric company, and saying good-bye to all the neighbors.

"Look at how big my muscle is," cried Stevie as he held up a thin little arm.

"Hey Stevie, want to play the alphabet game?" asked Collette. "Find an A on a license plate or a billboard."

"Can I play?" asked Laura. She pressed her teddy bear's face next to the window. "Barry can help."

"There's an A!" shouted Stevie as a large silver truck roared past.

"You cheater, Stevie!" cried Jeff. "There wasn't an A. That truck said Rod's Tires!"

Stevie flipped around in his seat to frown at Jeff. "Yes, sir! There was five A's and I saw them all."

"Maybe he saw the license plate, Jeff," Laura said sweetly. "Now find a B, Stevie. You're real good at this."

Jeff pulled his hat down and slumped in his seat. "I quit. I'm not playing with cheaters."

"No name calling," said their father. "We still have hours to go so let's try to get along. This is supposed to be our adventure together, remember?"

Collette and her mother sighed at the same time.

Five minutes of silence went by before Stevie asked if he could at least *see* the turnpike ticket. "I won't even touch it, Daddy. I just want to *see* it," he insisted.

"Don't let him, Dad," called up Jeff. "He'll lick it and then you'll be arrested for spreading Stevie germs!"

Stevie started to laugh. He licked his finger and

twisted in his seat as he tried to touch Jeff.

"Turn around, Stevie!" cried Collette. "Mom, Stevie is really giving me a headache."

Mrs. Murphy opened the glove compartment and handed Stevie a pack of gum. "You can be in charge of the gum, Stevie. Give everyone a piece."

"Don't bite mine, Stevie!" warned Laura.

Collette closed her eyes and frowned. Her family was *not* going to make a good impression on the island people. There were too many of them and they were too loud.

"Collette, do you want to start a story?" asked Mrs. Murphy.

Collette *didn't* want to tell a story. Laura and Stevie would keep interrupting and adding their two cents worth. The story would end up so stupid, it would be embarrassing.

"My head hurts," mumbled Collette. It was hard to argue with that complaint since no one could see inside your head to say, "No sir, look, everything is fine in your head so there's no way it can hurt. . . ."

"Should I sing?" offered Mr. Murphy.

"No!" the entire car shouted back. No offense to their father, but he couldn't sing at all. And he did it so loudly it was hard to ignore.

"I know," said Mrs. Murphy brightly. "Maybe now is a good time to tell you all about your new school."

Jeff groaned. He was still having a hard time understanding why you *had* to go to school on an island, which should be strictly for vacation.

"I love my teacher!" Laura said.

"You don't *know* your teacher, Laura," said Collette. For some reason, Laura's cheerfulness could really get on Collette's nerves sometimes.

"We've biked past the island school a hundred times during the summer," continued Mrs. Murphy. "I talked to Mr. Feris and you are all enrolled, ready to start next Monday. That will give us almost a week to settle into our new house."

"Good, that's when Sacred Heart starts." Collette was glad to know she would be getting exactly the same amount of education as Sarah and Marsha back in Pittsburgh. She really didn't want to fall behind and have to go to summer school.

Her father turned off the radio and started to laugh. "Did you tell them about the classes?"

Mrs. Murphy gave a bright smile. It was a forced smile, as if she sensed a little bit of trouble in the air. "Well, no. I thought I'd wait till . . . well, now."

Collette couldn't help but squirm in her seat.

What was so weird about the island classes that her mother wanted to hide the facts? Were the teachers mean? Or maybe the kids were so awful that the principal felt it his duty to warn any new students coming in.

"The new school is a little different from Sacred Heart," began her mother.

Collette's heart began to pound with a stronger and louder thump. It *must* be the kids. You could always fire a mean teacher, but you were stuck with the kids. The school laws said teachers had to give it their best shot till the kids were at least sixteen.

"How mean *are* the kids?" Collette asked. "Do they have policemen in the halls like some city schools?"

Mrs. Murphy turned and gave Collette a funny look. "The children on the island aren't mean, Collette."

"Sure they are," said Jeff, very matter-of-factly. "The whole island is kinda mean. Remember how quiet the people in the grocery store were to us? Nobody smiled or said thank you. They just smiled at each other!"

Collette nodded. The people living on the island seemed to like each other more than they liked the tourists. Except the librarians of course, Muriel and Marty. But librarians are nice to anyone who loves books.

"I'm sure the islanders get tired of the thoughtless tourists who come and litter and act crazy," said Mr. Murphy. "Remember, we only stay for two weeks, but the islanders have to put up with tourists for three months every summer!"

Mrs. Murphy sighed. "I know, Jay. But Jeff does have a point. Without the tourist trade, where would the islanders be?"

Mr. Murphy shrugged. "It's still their home. Having to depend on tourists for summer income probably adds to the problem."

"I hate them island people!" announced Stevie. "I'm never going to smile at them again."

"Stevie Murphy!" his mother scolded. "Don't you say a mean thing like that. The island is going to be our home for three months." She stared out the front window, then said, "We will become islanders?"

Collette gave a loud, short hoot. There was no way *she* was going to become an islander. She would stay there four months to be with her dad. But she was a Pittsburgher straight through.

"Tell the kids about the combined classes,"

urged Mr. Murphy. He pointed across Stevie. "Look — rest stop twenty miles."

Mrs. Murphy shifted in her seat and smiled back over the headrest. "Since the school is so small, they have combined first and second grade into one class. Same with third and fourth — "

"I'll be with *fifth*-graders?" Collette could hear the shrillness in her voice, but she couldn't help it. "You mean I'll be with . . . with little kids?"

Jeff reached out and jabbed Collette with his elbow. "I can whip you anyday, Collette. You're such a skinny shrimp; they'll put you in with Laura."

Laura grabbed Collette's arm and hugged it. "Will you come to my class, Collette? We could have so much fun!"

Collette twisted free from Laura's grasp and leaned closer to her mother. Was she the only one upset with the awful news? Surely Jeff wouldn't like being in with third-graders.

"Mom, this isn't going to work out. I *can't* be in the same room with fifth-graders. Sister Mary Elizabeth promised I could start Scholars this year because I make straight A's."

"Bragger!" snickered Jeff as he drove his finger into Collette's back. "You never get an A in gym,

Collette, and that's the most important class there is."

"You can start Scholars in January, Collette. I have already talked to Sister, and . . ."

"But Mom, if I don't get some real good teaching, then I'll . . . I'll lose some of my knowledge and . . . and the Scholar teachers will slam the door right in my face."

"On your nose?" asked Stevie. "Will they slam it on your nose, Collette?" He looked worried.

"Mom, I'm serious," Collette cried.

Mr. Murphy reached around and patted Collette's arm. "No one is going to be slamming any academic doors in your face, Collette. In fact, going to an island school will be a positive experience. There are only nine or ten in a class and . . ."

Collette threw herself back against the seat. "Sure Daddy. How positive can it be? Sacred Heart was going to be positive this year. I was finally going to be upstairs with the seventh- and eighth-graders, starting Scholars with Sarah . . ."

"You'll be upstairs at this little school, too, so stop being such a crybaby," Jeff said. "I don't know why you think being upstairs is such a big deal, anyway."

Their parents exchanged looks.

"What, what?" cried Collette. She had seen that look. Her parents knew something. "Tell me!"

"Well, at the island school, starting with fifth and sixth grades, all classes up to seniors are downstairs and the little children are upstairs."

"That's the dumbest thing I've ever heard of!" snapped Collette.

"I get to be an upstairs kid!" sang out Jeff.

"You can come in my upstairs room, Collette," offered Laura. Laura's eyes were getting bigger by the moment. Any second now she would squeeze them shut and cover her ears. Laura hated fighting. Even cowboys on television scared her.

"The teachers all sound wonderful," continued Mrs. Murphy. Her voice was racing as she tried to get to the better news about the school. "Children from the other islands either take the ferry or a small plane to school on Put-in-Bay each day. There isn't a single school bus."

"But I *like* school buses," said Stevie. "You tolded me I could ride a bus like the big guys when I went to kindergarten."

"I told you, not tolded, Stevie," his mother corrected him.

"Stevie will never learn to talk at this *dinky* school," Collette informed them. She sounded awful, using Marsha's words and not even caring. All the bad thoughts and feelings she had formed since the announcement of their four-month adventure were pouring out of her like a nasty leak.

"I do too know how to talk, Collette. Right, Jeff?"

"Right," replied Jeff. "Collette is a big grouch because she knows all those fifth-graders are going to pound her one. I heard that islanders throw Scholars into the lake."

"That's enough, Jeff." Mr. Murphy had lost every shred of cheerfulness. He turned the radio back on, loudly.

Laura closed her eyes, her neck shrinking down inside her sweatshirt. "I feel carsick . . ." she mumbled.

"Exit thirteen, nine more to go," said Mrs. Murphy in a very flat voice.

Nobody said anything back. Collette looked down at her fingernails. When was the fun going to start?

Chapter Three

"Here we are, children! Just a ferry ride away from your new home," Mrs. Murphy announced.

"I can see the ferry!" cried Laura. "It waited for us!" Mr. Murphy pulled the station wagon in line by Miller's Ferry.

Collette frowned. It was really irritating the way her parents kept calling the rented house, their new *home*. Their big red house on Browning Road was their *home*, the island house was just . . . just a rented house that belonged to complete strangers.

Jeff stuck his head out the window, watching as car after car drove aboard the black-and-white ferry. "Dad, I'm not getting on that ferry today.

They're letting too many cars on. It's going to sink before it passes Mouse Island."

Stevie crawled across his mother's lap and hung out the window. "Yeah, all them guys is going to sink, right Jeff?"

Mrs. Murphy pulled Stevie back inside the car. "Nobody is going to sink. Jeff, we have ridden this ferry for the past two summers. Four trips, Jeff. You should know by now how safe it is."

Collette unbuckled her seat belt and peered out the window. There were at least eight more cars ahead of theirs. It really was a full load.

"The islanders must have all brought their cars over for supplies," explained Mr. Murphy. "Groceries are a little less expensive at the Point grocery store on the mainland."

"Look, the sea gulls are waiting for us." Laura pointed to a large group of gulls, perched on rocks and railings. "Did you bring bread, Mommy?"

Mrs. Murphy held up a plastic bag filled with crusts. "I saved everyone's leftovers from lunch."

Jeff opened the door and got out. "Well, *I'm* not getting on the ferry. Last time there were only four or five cars. Look at that thing! There's an ice truck, a beer truck, and a zillion other cars."

"I don't like that ferry." Stevie hopped off the

front seat and climbed out to stand beside Jeff. "Me and Jeff are going to take the bus to that island."

Laura opened her door and got out. "You can't take the bus, Stevie. Buses can't drive on water, right, Daddy?"

Mr. Murphy turned off the engine, leaving the keys in the ignition. "Right, Shortiecake—now, the men will drive the car on. Kids, stay here because I'm going to take the bikes off and you can walk them onto the ferry."

Stevie zoomed around Jeff and Laura. "I'm going to *race* my bike on!"

Mrs. Murphy hurried out of the car, stopping Stevie by the back of his shirt. "Listen, Stevie. I've already explained this to you. The ferrymen said you *must* walk the bike on. It's a very important rule."

Mr. Murphy held out a hand and helped Collette out from the backseat. He pulled her close and gave her a quick hug. "Look at that blue sky, Peanut. You don't get skies like that in Pittsburgh. Give your old dad a smile."

Collette gave her dad a hug back. Her head was still pounding from the four-hour car ride.

Mr. Murphy handed Collette three twenty-dollar bills. "Get our tickets while I get the bikes off the rack. Tell them one car, two adults, three kids. I think Stevie is free."

Collette glanced over at Stevie as he scrambled over the top of the car. They should charge double for Stevie. He was the one who required the most watching.

When Collette returned with the tickets, the last bike was leaning against the car.

"Daddy, if the ferry *does* sink, will you have time to start blowing up my floating ring?" Laura gripped the handlebars of her pink bike. "Maybe we should blow it up now!"

Collette followed Laura's gaze out across the choppy green water.

"The ferry is *not* going to sink!" said her mother in a very final voice.

Jeff walked his bike a little closer. "Yeah, but how do you *know* that, Mom? I mean, if people knew a ferry was going to sink, they wouldn't get on it. Then no ferry in the whole world would sink, right, Dad?"

Mr. Murphy took the tickets and his change. "The ferry is not going to sink so that's the end of it. Now, children, walk the bikes down to the gate and wait there for your mother and me. I'll take Stevie's bike down for him."

"No fair," cried Stevie. He reached out and held onto his bike. "I'm as strong as the big guys!"

"You are not," laughed Jeff as he walked past. "Shrimp-face."

Stevie sat down on the pavement, his feet sticking straight out. "That's it. I'm not going then. Leave me here all by myself for robber men."

"Get up off that tar!" snapped Mrs. Murphy. "Oh, Stevie. Look at your jeans."

"I want to walk my bike!" sobbed Stevie. "I'm big!"

"Stevie, get up and you can walk my bike," offered Laura. "No one will laugh at you 'cause it's pink."

"No Laura!" Mr. Murphy grumbled. "Stay out of this, please. I don't want Stevie walking *any* bike. I don't care *what* color it is!"

Collette reached over and patted Laura as two fat tears rolled down her face. Laura had only been trying to help.

Stevie could sure cause a lot of trouble. And he was so loud. Probably the loudest five-year-old in the world.

"Get up, Stevie!" ordered Collette. Everyone who walked by was watching the Murphy family, probably wondering who such noisy, rude people were.

Mr. Murphy yanked Stevie up. "You listen to your mother, do you understand?"

Stevie nodded, his face red and smeared with dirty tears.

"Bikers first!" shouted the large man in a white T-shirt. "Keep to the right and have your ticket ready."

"Let's go upstairs and watch the sea gulls, Stevie," suggested Mrs. Murphy. "Here, you can hold the bread for Mommy."

Stevie shook his head, sniffing. "I want to ride my bike like a big guy. Babies hold bread bags."

Mr. Murphy gave an exasperated sigh and shoved the bike in Stevie's direction. "I give up. The ferry is going to leave before I can get you people on board. Here, Stevie. Walk the bike."

"Yippee!" cried Stevie. He ran over and hugged Mr. Murphy's leg. "You're the best daddy!"

Collette laughed, glad they could finally stop arguing about the bike. It seemed some conversations never got anywhere in her family.

A large lady nudged her friend as she walked

past. They both frowned as Stevie gripped his red handlebars and hurried down the wide cement drive leading to the ferry.

"In my day, parents stuck to their guns more," the larger lady said. She looked right at Mr. Murphy as she spoke, as though her words might help him rethink his decision.

"It's no wonder kids today are the way they are, Gert," added her friend. She shifted her grocery bag so she could get a better look at Mrs. Murphy. "I read about a ten-year-old that up and stabbed his parents as they slept."

Collette drew herself up, walking her bike in the most perfect way possible. What do you two ladies know? They had not been in the Murphy car for the past four hours, listening to four grouchy, hungry kids.

All the ladies knew was that a new bunch of tourists were coming to their island. You could tell the ladies were islanders, and both of them looked annoyed that someone as noisy as Stevie was heading for Put-in-Bay.

"Look at how careful I am!" shouted Stevie. "Daddy, look at how good I am."

"Daddy, the chain fell off my bike again," cried Laura. Mr. Murphy groaned, handing his wife the tickets. "Oh, great. Kate, can you fix the chain? I'll be there in a second."

"I'll go help with Stevie," offered Collette. She said it loud enough that the two island ladies turned around. The Murphys may be loud but at least they stuck together, thought Collette. She shook back her blonde hair and marched proudly past the ladies.

"Watch this, Collette," cried Stevie as she walked up beside him.

Stevie whacked up the kickstand and hopped onto his bike, the bag of bread crusts sticking out of his back pocket.

"Stevie. Daddy told you to *walk* the bike down!"

Stevie gave Collette a puzzled stare before he zoomed toward the railing. "I did walk it down. But I'm already down now. It's OK to ride where it's flat. Watch my trick, Collette."

"Get back here, Stevie!" shouted Collette. She gripped her bike and searched the crowd of passengers.

Where was that kid? Collette could hear Stevie's happy hoots of freedom, but she couldn't spot the small, red two-wheeler, or see Stevie's mop of curly blond hair.

"You better get that little brother of yours and

tie him down somewheres safe," advised the large lady called Gert as she stopped beside Collette. She shifted her bag from her left to right hip. "Dogs have to be leashed on the ferry, and if you ask me, that brother of yours should be on one, too."

Gert's friend started to laugh.

Collette's throat started to tighten. She looked at the large lady's fuzzy red hair and the large square teeth shining back at her. Why didn't she offer to help if she had so much good advice to give?

Couldn't they see Collette was trying? Did the ladies think she enjoyed having perfect strangers make fun of her family?

The ladies both gave identical sighs, their brown bags rising and falling in unison.

"Well Gert, what do you expect from *tourons*?"

Collette gave her bike an angry push ahead. She scraped her ankle with the kickstand, but didn't even bend over to see how bad it was.

Tourons? What was a touron? Did those awful ladies think Collette was a relative of some terrible family on the island named Touron?

"Stevie Murphy!" Collette hollered again and again. There, let both of those busybody ladies know that she wasn't a Touron. She was a Murphy, a Murphy from Pittsburgh.

"Hey Collette, watch my trick!" Stevie whizzed out of nowhere, past Collette and headed toward the wide red ramp. "Marsha taught me this trick!"

"Stevie!" Collette dropped her bike and took off after Stevie, barreling recklessly through the crowd. She had to catch Stevie before he got any closer to the rope separating the ramp from the lake.

"Stevie! Stephen!!" Mr. Murphy shouted as he ran down the length of the drive toward the ferry. "Stop, Stevie!"

"Watch out, kid!" yelled a huge man. He pulled back hard on the thick leather leashes of his two golden retrievers, yanking both startled dogs out of Stevie's way.

Stevie stood up on his pedals, twisting his head to look back at the barking dogs. "Sorry dogs. I wasn't going to bump you!"

As the ferry gave three long toots, Stevie turned back. Collette didn't even have time to scream before Stevie smashed into the thick wooden post of the gate leading to the ferry.

The bike skidded to the left, throwing Stevie against a ferry attendant. He reached down and yanked Stevie up, pulling him close. The bike clattered across the pavement like a giant crab before it hurtled out across the water, sinking front tire first into Lake Erie.

"My bike!" screamed Stevie, scrambling out of the attendant's arms.

Mr. Murphy reached Stevie before he could get any closer to the water. He picked him up, searching Stevie's face and wiggling both arms up and down.

"Daddy, go get my bike. It's drowning!"

"Serves that child right if you ask me," muttered Gert. She pushed past Collette and handed the attendant her ticket.

Three more toots drowned out Stevie's cries for a moment. The line filed past Collette; no one even slowed down to offer assistance.

Behind her, Collette could hear Laura, Jeff, and her mother clambering down the hill with their bikes.

Collette slowed to a snail's pace. With any luck, the ferry would take off without them.

Chapter Four

"Mom, can't you make Stevie stop crying?" begged Collette. "My head feels like it's going to explode!"

Mrs. Murphy gave Stevie another pat on his back and made a few hushing sounds. She had been doing this for the past thirty minutes and nothing had worked.

"Yeah, be quiet Stevie!" ordered Jeff. "The whole ferry just took a vote and you're a pain in the neck."

"Well Jeff, how would you feel if your very favorite bike just drowned in the lake?" asked Laura quietly. "I think Stevie should be allowed to cry for a whole week if he wants to, right, Mommy?"

Mrs. Murphy looked out across the lake and

just shook her head. "Don't give him any ideas, Laura."

Collette gently shook Stevie's arm. "Listen, Stevie, we all feel bad about your bike sinking . . ."

Stevie sobbed louder than ever, burying his wet face into his mother's white blouse. "It sank all the way to the bottom!"

"But, I told you to walk and you insisted on riding your bike so this is what happens," continued Collette. "You should have listened to Daddy's first plan and . . ."

"I want my bike!" wailed Stevie as he pointed out across the railing. "Make them turn the ferry around, Collette, and look for my bike."

"Need any help?"

Collette looked up, shielding her eyes against the sun. A tall, muscular boy with thick blond hair smiled down at her and Stevie.

"I saw what happened back at the dock. Too bad about the bike." He knelt down on one knee in front of Stevie! "Hey — you really wiped out back there."

Stevie looked up, wiping both eyes. "It was my bike."

"No fooling," muttered Jeff. He looked embarrassed to be with his family because of all the fuss Stevie was making.

The ferry gave three loud blasts as it neared the dock of Put-in-Bay.

Mrs. Murphy rubbed her temples and made a face. "Does the captain have to blast his horn so often?"

The boy sat down on the bench next to Collette and laughed. "He's just trying to impress the tourons."

"The Tourons . . . ?" Collette searched the crowded ferry, looking for a wildly dressed, loud-mouthed family. "Do the Tourons live on the island?"

The boy studied Collette for a second. His face grew slightly red. "Nah, it was just a dumb joke, that's all."

Stevie slid slowly off his mother's lap, sitting next to the boy on the bench. "Do they have bike stores on the island?"

The boy thought for a second, then shook his head. "I don't think so."

Stevie's face fell, his small shoulders slumped against the back of the bench.

"Stevie, come and help me feed the sea gulls," Laura laughed from the railing. "Trick or treat, birdies," she called as she flung a handful of bread crumbs out across the water.

A few gulls caught the bread in their beaks, the other crumbs sailed slowly to the surface of the water.

"Trick or treat — trick or treat!" shouted Laura.

Collette felt a prick of homesickness again. Halloween — trick or treat. This year she wouldn't be able to rush across the street, holding the hem of her costume in one hand and makeup in the other so she and Marsha could do each other's faces.

"Loan me one of your old pillowcases for my candy," Marsha would insist each year. "Our pillowcases are too fancy for chocolate stains."

Collette smiled. The longer she was away from Browning Road, the more she remembered the fun, good parts of Marsha.

"My bike was red," Stevie confided to the boy in a sad voice.

The boy nodded. He looked sad, too. "I saw it just before it hit the lake. It sure went fast."

A little flicker of light appeared in Stevie's pale blue eyes. "Was it the fastest bike in the world?"

"Oh brother!" groaned Jeff. He pushed his baseball cap down over his eyes and scooted further down on the bench. "It was your own fault, Stevie. If you had listened to Dad you would still have your bike."

"I was being real good and careful!" yelled Stevie. He leaned across the tall boy and shook his fist at Jeff. "Nothing was my fault!"

The boy looked across at Collette and tried to hide a smile.

"I was being real good!" Stevie insisted in his loud voice.

Collette smiled back. Actually the Murphys had already made such an awful impression on the whole boat it didn't matter anymore.

Laura walked back to them, looking thoughtful. "I think Stevie *thought* he was being good, but that's because he just gets into a lot of trouble without trying to."

"No sir!" Stevie insisted. He looked around the ferry for a second.

"That old lady over there tripped me when I turned to look at those big dogs. She pushed me."

Collette followed Stevie's stubby finger to the bench. The large lady named Gert and her friend scowled back at Stevie, their mouths pushed into identical pincushions of disgust.

"Stevie!" said Mrs. Murphy quickly. She

reached out, but Stevie moved ahead to the bench on which the two women sat.

"This one!" continued Stevie, taking a step closer and bringing a finger right up to Gert's face. "This fatter one."

"Stevie Murphy!" his mother cried, hurrying over. She took Stevie by the arm and pulled him back. "I am terribly sorry. My little boy is very upset over losing his bike in the lake."

"I was not anywhere near your child," insisted Gert.

The thinner woman shoved her glasses up a notch and nodded.

Collette noticed her mother's cheeks grew pinker as she led Stevie back to their bench.

The boy they'd been talking to stood up and stuck out his hand.

"Hi, I'm Brian Kepler. I live on the island. Don't mind Gert and Annie. They're both really nice once you get to know them."

Mrs. Murphy smiled and shook his hand. "I'm sure they are. Hi, I'm Mrs. Murphy and this is Laura, Jeff, Stevie, and Collette."

Stevie stepped forward and slapped Brian a high five.

"Hey buddy!" laughed Brian.

Collette smiled, glad Stevie was being so sweet. He was a nice little kid. He didn't *try* to get in trouble all the time; he just did. Brian was talking to Stevie, telling him how sorry he was about his bike. Brian looked about Collette's age. Maybe they would be in the same class on the island. That would be great.

"And now I won't have a bike," said Stevie, shaking his head.

"We'll see if we can rent you one on the island for a few months, Stevie," offered Collette. "And I can ride you on the back of mine sometimes, too."

Brian looked up and smiled at Collette, nodding his head. "Yeah, and since you won't have a bike to walk off the ferry, you can help me out, old buddy."

Brian gently lifted a green canvas backpack from the floor and set it on Stevie's lap. "Hold on, Stevie. My cat Mertze is inside. She's pregnant and I just took her to Port Clinton for a checkup. She isn't feeling too well."

"Seasick," suggested Stevie wisely.

Brian nodded. "I have to carry a bag of groceries for my mom, so it would be a big help if you carried Mertze off the ferry for me. Can you handle that?"

Stevie held up his arm and made a muscle. "Look how strong I am."

Mrs. Murphy and Collette both looked at the steep, gray metal steps leading to the lower deck.

"Brian, Stevie would love to help you, but those steps are awfully steep," cautioned Mrs. Murphy.

Jeff shoved his baseball cap down. "Yeah, and Stevie is awfully clumsy."

The ferry tooted again and Brian stood up. "I'll be right in front of him. He's a strong guy. Just watch the first step, Stevie. It's a long one."

Collette and her mother smiled at each other as Stevie cradled the sack and stood up to stand next to Brian.

"Brian, your cat is meowing that she loves me."

A few passengers looked up at Stevie and smiled. It was a good thing that God had made Stevie so cute with his bright blue eyes and blond curls. It made up for his big mouth.

Mrs. Murphy put her arm around Collette and took Laura's hand. "See how nice the islanders can be? Things are going to work out perfectly."

"Oh, Mom," said Collette with a grin. Her mother thought she had to underline things or her kids wouldn't get the message.

"Jeff, remind Daddy we have to stop at the store

for bottled water and food for tonight," said Mrs. Murphy.

"I am so hungry," Collette said. Being on the island always made her extra hungry. She looked across the lake. Put-in-Bay was getting closer. The sun was halfway down, radiating reddish orange stripes across the sky. Put-in-Bay was so pretty, prettier than Pittsburgh.

"Maybe I'll pick up a turkey for tomorrow night and we can have sandwiches and a casserole from it," Mrs. Murphy suggested.

Behind her, Collette could hear Gert and Annie start to whisper.

"Remind me to get lunch bags and drink boxes for school next week," she continued. "We didn't have room for any groceries in the car."

Gert reached out and tapped Collette's mother on the arm. "You should have done all your shopping at the Point before you got on the ferry, miss."

Mrs. Murphy smiled back. "We were too rushed and . . ."

Gert started to explain. "The grocery store on the island burned down last May. We've got a trailer set up now till we can build a new store, but there isn't a whole lot there. Just enough for the islanders to get by."

"That's terrible," said Mrs. Murphy. "It was such a lovely store. I hope nobody was hurt!"

Gert shook her head. "A few burns, that's all. The trees across the street got scorched, and the arcade above the store burned, too. We feel blessed that the whole street didn't go up like a string of firecrackers."

"That's awful," said Collette. "Mom, why didn't anyone tell us about the fire?"

Gert gave a small shrug. "Guess nobody on the island remembered you were coming, miss."

Collette leaned back against the wall and let the ladies past. She felt a bitter taste in her mouth. What if Gert was right?

Maybe nobody on the whole island cared that the Murphys were coming.

Chapter Five

"But this can't be the house!" Collette cried. She leaned her head out the window to get a better look. "It's so . . . so little! Maybe you turned onto the wrong street, Daddy."

The station wagon drove up to a squat, dark green house and pulled slowly into the gravel drive. Mrs. Murphy picked up an envelope from the dashboard.

"Fourteen Chestnut Lane. This is it."

Jeff pounded his fist into his mitt. "Yeah, well where are the other thirteen houses? We are in the middle of nowhere."

"I see a yellow house right through the trees," Laura pointed out. "That house looks prettier. Can we trade, Mommy?"

"This house really does look small, Jay," Mrs. Murphy said carefully. "Are you sure the real estate agent knows we have four children?" She tried to smile, but Mr. Murphy did not smile back. He studied the house. "He said it has three bedrooms, one bath."

"One bath?" asked Jeff. "Sure — I bet it's out back."

Mr. Murphy finally smiled. "Come on, troops. This is our adventure, remember?"

Laura leaned forward and hugged her father's neck. "I love this house, Daddy. It looks just like a doll's house."

Mrs. Murphy opened the car door and got out. "It's not even two stories, just a story and a half."

"Maybe it's bigger on the inside," suggested Collette hopefully.

"Home sweet home!" announced Mr. Murphy in a train conductor's voice. "Let's grab a few suitcases and get unpacked."

Collette reached for the box of blankets. She would help all she could. But she knew that the awful-looking house in front of them would never stand for home sweet home.

Laura scrambled out of her side of the car and ran across the grass to a small cement birdbath.

She bent down and picked up a large pinecone and started splashing the dirty water out.

"Collette, look. A little birdbath to match the little house. Want to help me clean it up and put in fresh water for the birds?"

"Wait till we unload the car, Laura," Collette called back. She reached inside the car and took a box filled with towels. The whole car was filled with boxes and suitcases: it would take forever to unpack.

Collette looked around the large yard, her neck craning to see the tops of the tall pine trees. She could hardly wait to start exploring. Chestnut Lane was off the regular bike route they used during their summer vacations. It looked fun to explore.

She carried the box up the front walk, staring at the house. Two large windows were on either side of the dark wooden door, and a circular window was above it, staring down at Collette like the eye of a cyclops.

"I like this house, don't you, Collette?" asked Stevie. "It looks like the house where the three bears live."

Jeff snorted, waving his arm through the cobwebs that stretched across the front entrance.

"Yeah, and I bet they're still inside, too. Boy, Dad, this house is covered with spiderwebs. I think we got ripped off on this place."

Collette laughed. "Jeff, remember how we had to knock the spiderwebs off our bikes every morning last summer? Spiders must love islands."

Mr. Murphy laughed, too. He swung another bike down from the rack. "This house looks fine. It's been vacant for almost a year, so you have to expect a little dust."

Mrs. Murphy set a suitcase down and wiped her hands together. "I'm not worried about the dust, but I can't believe the real estate man forgot to tell us the grocery store burned down."

Stevie nodded. "Brian said they let all the kids from the school run down to watch the fire. Brian said my teacher is nice."

"I guess I'll have to take the car back over on the ferry and load it up with groceries at the Point," Mrs. Murphy continued. She sat down on the edge of a suitcase and rubbed her forehead.

"Let's go inside and see how pretty the house is," said Collette. She tried to sound as cheerful as possible.

Jeff put his hands on his hips and studied the yard. "Hey Dad, where's the basketball hoop?

Didn't you tell the real estate guy we needed a hoop?"

Stevie put his hands on his hips, too. "Yeah, and them guys took away the cement, too. How can you bounce the basketball on stones, Jeff?"

Jeff groaned and tossed his basketball into the bushes. "Great! I'll never make the fourth-grade team when we get back if I can't practice. I'm already going to miss the September clinic, and. . . ."

Collette knew how much basketball meant to Jeff. He was always bouncing a ball, dribbling it through his legs like the older boys did.

"Jeff, I bet there's a hoop at the elementary school," said Collette.

Mr. Murphy took down the last bike and pulled the keys out of his back pocket. "We were really lucky to get this place at all. Not very many of the rentals have a furnace."

Mrs. Murphy stood up and smiled. "I think it's going to be fine, just fine once we get it . . . cleaned up a little."

Collette gripped her box more tightly and nodded, glad that her family was being more positive. After all, they were over two hundred miles from home. That meant they had to stick together.

"Well, if I don't make the team next year, I'm quitting school," grumbled Jeff, walking towards the bushes and his ball.

Stevie started hopping around the porch. "Hurry up with them keys, Daddy. I really have to go to the bathroom."

"I'm coming," his father said. He studied the key ring. "Now one key is for the shed around back, one for the side door, and maybe this one is . . ."

"Really, hurry!" called Stevie, running around in a little circle. "I have to go *right now!*"

"Spiders are on me!" cried Laura, holding both hands out as she raced around the side of the house. "I tried to hang up a birdhouse and . . . oh, get them off my head!"

Collette dropped her box and ran with her mother to Laura. Both of them pulled the sticky webs from Laura's blonde hair.

"What about me?" cried Stevie. "I have to go to the bathroom!"

Collette glanced over her shoulder as her father unlocked the door and hurried inside with Stevie.

"I hate spiders," shouted Laura, shivering all over. "You can't even tell if they're looking at you!"

"Stand still, Laura!" said Collette. "And stop

yelling. The whole island is going to hear us! I am so embarrassed!"

Mrs. Murphy looked across at Collette and winked. "I think they already know we've landed, honey."

"Let's go inside and wash our hands," suggested Collette. "Then we can set up our room, okay, Laura?"

Collette tried to keep smiling, but she remembered from past vacations that sometimes the water pipes clanged at first, coughing and spitting for the first few minutes, and then rusty-colored water would splash out. And the rooms would need to be dusted and swept. Collette's mother had packed a whole box filled with cleaning stuff and would make everyone pitch in and help. Collette sighed — it would be awhile before the house was ready for the Murphys.

As soon as she walked into the living room, she felt slightly embarrassed, as though she had insulted someone who'd turned out to be very nice. The living room, with its bright white walls and wooden trim, was beautiful. Two burgundy-and-white checked loveseats faced each other in front of the fireplace, with a tall navy chair and matching footstool alongside. Collette walked closer and set her box down on the large wooden coffee table, which had been made from a giant wire spool.

"Wow, this is so pretty!" cried Collette, sinking into the navy chair and sticking her legs out on the footstool.

"It's lovely," her mother said. She and Laura sat on the loveseat and grinned.

"Can we have a fire tonight?" asked Collette.

Her mother nodded. "If Daddy doesn't fall asleep too soon." She stood up. "Let's check out the kitchen . . . in case we ever locate some food!"

Collette felt her good mood growing. This house was small, but it was really pretty. She walked to the front window and looked out. Even the front yard looked nicer when you looked at it from inside the house. Collette tapped on the window and waved to her father as he carried another load of boxes up the walk.

"Which way to the kitchen?" asked her father from the doorway. He held a large cardboard box filled with paper plates and cups.

"Isn't this nice?" said her mother as she sat on the couch. "Let me sit here a week and recover from that trip. I don't ever want to get back in that car."

Mr. Murphy walked back in and sat beside his

wife. He grabbed her hand and gave it a kiss. "A real honeymoon getaway, Kate."

Collette laughed. "With four kids to chaperone."

Her father stood up and stuck his head up the fireplace opening. "Looks OK. We'll have a fire next month when things cool down. I did pack my old jigsaw for kindling wood. We can start stacking it by the red shed."

Laura stomped down the stairs, hands on her hips. "Stevie has been in the bathroom for too long and he won't come out, Daddy, and I have spiderwebs all over my fingers."

Mr. Murphy went to the bottom of the steps and called up. "Stevie, Laura has to wash her hands. Let her in."

"I don't like this toilet!" called Stevie from the other side of the door. "There's too much water."

Mr. and Mrs. Murphy exchanged horrified looks before they both took off up the stairs.

"I didn't do it!" cried Stevie as his father started to yell. "All that water just exploded when I flushed."

"Find a bucket, get a mop!" Mr. Murphy barked from the top of the stairs. Mrs. Murphy hurried past, her face red and tired looking.

"Would somebody wake me up and tell me this

is all a bad dream," she muttered as she passed.

Collette went into the kitchen, opening cabinets and looking for rags for her dad. She opened a cabinet without a handle, frowning at the plastic plates, mismatched glasses, and tea-stained cups. Tourist stuff. Leftover things from someone else's kitchen. Dinner plates with orange faded flowers crisscrossed with knife slashes.

Only six dinner plates here. Collette closed the cabinet. Oh well, six plates would be plenty for the next few months.

"Look at what I picked, Collette!" Laura thrust up a fistful of flowers for Collette to smell. "The whole backyard is filled with flowers!"

Mrs. Murphy hurried into the kitchen, the wet mop dripping a crooked stream behind her. "Girls, take the cardboard box marked 'Linens' upstairs, please. Collette, you and Laura take the double bed and the boys can have the bunk beds."

"What? Mom, I *cannot* sleep with Laura!" Collette blurted out. "She sleeps with too many stuffed animals and there is no room left for me. Besides, she flops all over the bed. . . ."

"I do not flop, Collette." Laura smacked the goldenrod down so hard the yellow pollen sprayed across the counter.

"Yes you do. And you slurp on your thumb and . . ." Collette shook her head. "This is not going to work out."

"Collette, I can't let Stevie and Jeff sleep in the same bed. Stevie would keep Jeff up all night trying to wrestle."

"Thanks a lot, Mom," Collette's voice thinned to a whine. "It's all right for *me* to be up all night with Laura, but not Jeff." Collette knew she was being awful, but she couldn't help it.

She tried to look as wounded as possible. It was bad enough she had to share a room with Laura back in Pittsburgh, but at least she had a shred of privacy by being up in the top bunk. Now she had to share half a room and half a bed with Laura and her zillion stuffed animals.

"Take the box up and we can talk about this later." Mrs. Murphy set the box down and rubbed her back. She looked tired and wore the same face she had used on the cobwebs and toilet.

Laura picked up her flowers and smiled. "Collette, you can have most of the bed, OK? I'm not that big, yet."

Collette smiled back and followed Laura out of the kitchen. "Thanks. And you don't really flop too much. Maybe we could put most of your stuffed animals on top of the dresser, Laura. They could guard us."

"Yeah," Laura agreed. "Guard us from spiders."

"You carry the towels and I'll carry the box, Laura."

Collette could see her dad scowling as he peered into the back of the toilet tank. His brand-new white tennis shoes were soaked.

"Come and get your sheets, boys!" Collette called out as she set the box on top of her bed.

Both boys were already in their small room, quietly sitting side by side on the bottom bunk.

Even after the long, noisy car ride up, the stillness in their room worried Collette. Her brothers were always in motion: chasing, wrestling, fighting, and laughing.

Now they were absolutely quiet. They looked so homesick. At home there were so many kids on their street that they could always find someone who wanted to play kickball or freeze tag.

Collette carried in some blue sheets and laid them on the small green dresser. "Mom wants you to make your beds, boys."

"I miss my old bed," said Stevie slowly. "This bed smells like a doctor's office."

Collette smiled. "Mom sprayed it. Hurry up and then we can go exploring."

As Collette turned back into the hall, she saw her mother running up the stairs. "Jay, you better come down here. The handle of the refrigerator just came off in my hand. The small amount of food we had is now locked inside."

From the bathroom, Collette could hear her father give a grunt. More of a growl, really.

"Hey, how can I get food?" asked Stevie, running out from his room. "I think I'm hungry right now."

Collette scooted down the hall and went into her room. Just when she thought things were calming down, another emergency popped up. She closed her door and smiled at her little room. The small cyclops window seemed to be watching her for a reaction.

"This is nice," said Collette happily. She set her sheets on the double bed, running her hand across the high wooden headboard. "We just need a little air in here."

Collette walked over and pushed hard against the heavy brass handle. With a mighty shove, the window finally opened, large flakes of yellow paint falling to the floor.

A gentle breeze blew in, bringing with it the fresh smell of spruce and cut grass. Collette stuck her head out further, looking down at the station wagon, surrounded by boxes and suitcases. It would take forever to bring everything in and put it away.

Collette saw Laura back outside by the birdbath, splashing out the water and talking to herself. Beyond the car, Collette saw her mother and Stevie pointing toward the lake. They were smiling.

Collette took in a deep breath, glad to be out of the car and off the ferry. Today had been long and hectic, but tomorrow was just around the corner and it would be better, Collette just knew it. Tomorrow the island adventure would begin.

Tomorrow she would bike alongside the lake, down Main Street, by the monument, and stop to see the boats at the marina. That was something she couldn't do in Pittsburgh.

Collette took in a deep breath of sun and island pine. The next few months on the island would be wonderful, a chance to love Put-in-Bay even more.

Chapter Six

Dear Sarah,

I am finally finished unpacking. I still have to share a room with Laura. The room is so small!!! So far things are pretty boring. My mom made me help clean the kitchen . . . gross! . . . and Laura was afraid of the moon looking in our round window so she kept waking me up all night. The only exciting part was meeting a nice boy on the ferry. He is coming over in a couple of minutes to show Jeff where he can play basketball. He is cute but he is only a friend, Sarah, so don't start thinking. . . .

P.S. His name is Brian.

"Collette, if you're coming, come on!" Jeff shouted up the stairs. "Brian is outside!"

Collette folded her letter in half and stuck it under a shoe box filled with pens and markers. She could finish it after dinner. By then she would have a whole full day of news. Maybe Brian had a sister, or a cousin who would be going into the sixth grade. A possible friend . . .

"Come on, Collette!" Laura stood in the doorway, breathless. "Brian brought his cat. He said that Stevie and me can be helpers till the kittens are born. Isn't Brian nice, Collette?"

As soon as Collette stood up, her mother rushed in holding a bag. "Here, I packed some apples and pretzels for a snack. You're going with the kids, aren't you, Collette?"

Collette nodded, trying not to look too eager. She didn't want her mother to think she was going because she liked Brian as a cute boy. He *was* a boy, and he *was* cute, really cute. But he was just a friend, the only friend any of the Murphys had on the island. And judging from the way everyone had treated them on the ferry, and later at the grocery store in the trailer when they stopped for supplies, he might be the only friend they *would* have for the next four months.

"Keep an eye on Stevie, Collette. All this water makes me a little nervous. You know how crazy he is." Mrs. Murphy fished in the pocket of her jean skirt and handed Collette a few folded dollar bills. "Treat everyone, especially Brian, to a cone at Frosty's. He was so nice to Stevie at the ferry yesterday."

Laura pulled on her mother's skirt. "Brian said he would take us all into town to watch the men take the merry-go-round apart. They take each horse off, each dog off, and even the red rooster, and they pack them in a special crate until May." Laura paused. "Then the men take all the clothes and gifts out of the gift stores so no robber men can break a window and steal everything. Isn't that a smart idea?"

"Don't any stores stay open after the Labor Day events end?" Mrs. Murphy looked worried. "Sounds like a ghost town."

"Hey, don't say that! It still stays pretty wild around here."

Collette jumped, turning to see Brian standing in the doorway, stroking Mertze's yellow fur. "Tripper's restaurant stays open, the post office, school, and the grocery store."

"The grocery *trailer* you mean," laughed Jeff.

"They only have two aisles in that store." Jeff laughed again. "How tiny."

Collette looked at Brian. He wasn't laughing. To an islander, a grocery trailer was better than no grocery.

Laura tugged on his sleeve. "Your island is just like Rip Van Winkle's town that fell asleep."

"Rip fell asleep, not the town," corrected Collette.

"And then the town wakes up and all the stores are open and the merry-go-round gets unpacked and it's a big party." Laura smiled at everyone.

"Where . . . I mean, what happens to the employees when everything closes, Brian?" asked Mrs. Murphy. "Do they take jobs on the mainland?"

"A lot of people are unemployed during the winter season," said Brian very matter-of-factly. "Once the lake freezes, you couldn't go to work on the mainland even if you had a job, unless you flew."

"Wow," said Jeff. "Lots of steelworkers had to get new jobs in Pittsburgh. My friend's dad had to look a long time for a new job."

Brian nodded. "Ice fishing keeps a lot of people busy. Boy, you should see some of the ice shacks."

"A shack right on top of the ice?" asked Stevie. "Won't they sink, like my bike?"

Everyone laughed. "The ice is too thick, Stevie. In fact, sometimes people drive cars straight across to another island."

Mrs. Murphy's eyes grew as large as Stevie's. "Boy, do I feel like a tourist!"

Brian laughed. "Better than a touron!"

Collette looked up. Touron. Who in the world were those awful people everyone on the island made fun of?

"Some ladies on the ferry thought we were related to the Tourons," said Collette. "What arc they like? Are they nice?"

Brian's face got as red as his flannel shirt. "Forget it. They probably didn't mean a thing."

Collette stood beside him, smiling. "Come on. I won't get mad. Are they real loud, or do they just have a lot of kids?"

Brian petted his cat for several minutes before he looked up. "It's just an island term, Collette. Don't take it too seriously."

"What does it mean?" asked her mother.

Brian scratched behind Mertze's ear for another minute. "Touron is short for a summer person — half tourist, half moron . . . touron."

Collette gulped. The ferry people thought the Murphys were . . . were dumb tourists who didn't know how to act on Put-in-Bay?

"My uncle has a real cool ice shack," began Brian. "It has a bench inside, a potbellied stove, and shelves filled with snack food and soda. I can show you guys if you want to see it. And they have real old ice shacks in the Historical Museum across from the gas station."

Mrs. Murphy laughed. "After all, there *is* only *one* gas station on the island. I bet he's a popular guy."

Collette crossed her arms, a frown still on her face. Was it her imagination or was she the only one who was insulted that the Murphys were thought of as . . . as tourons! That was a great nickname to walk into school with on Monday.

"Can I go fishing for ice with your uncle?" asked Stevie. "I love ice cream."

"Stevie!" Collette groaned. Honestly, how could the Murphys show they were smart, *untourony* people with Stevie asking dumb questions like that?

Brian laughed. "You cut through the ice, Buddy. Then you try and catch fish. By the end of November, the lake might already be frozen over. The ferry closes down November fifteenth or so. I'll ask my uncle if we can go sometime."

"Cool!" said Jeff. He looked real excited. "What a huge ice hockey field!"

"Wait a minute," cried Collette suddenly. "I bet my dad doesn't know about the lake freezing. He was planning on taking the ferry to get to court each day. What if he gets stranded? The judge will let the other side win."

Brian didn't seem the least bit worried. "People who can afford it take the planes when the lake freezes. It's no big deal. Besides, the lake doesn't always freeze before Christmas. Last year Captain Charlie brought back a supply of freshly cut Christmas trees from the mainland."

"We'll be home by Christmas. We usually get the biggest tree we can find for our living room." Collette wanted Brian to know that they did have a nice house in Pittsburgh, and that nobody there would ever think of calling the Murphys a bunch of tourons. "We have three stories to our house there."

Her mother gave Collette a look. "Well, we don't use the third floor for much, storage, mostly."

"But we have it. Two more bedrooms and a bath," insisted Collette.

Brian didn't look impressed. He just smiled.

"Sounds nice. Well, we better get going. You guys are invited to stay for lunch. My mom left a pot of chili."

"Great!" said Jeff. "I love chili."

Collette handed Stevie his sweatshirt. "Put it on, Stevie. Mind if I come, Brian? My mom likes me to keep an eye on Stevie."

"Great — come on. I'll show you a new place for pinecones. My mom makes great wreaths every year."

"Maybe she could show me how to make them," suggested Mrs. Murphy. Collette was surprised to hear the eagerness in her mother's voice. Maybe her mother was already feeling a little homesick for her friends, too.

Once outside, Stevie started to whine. "Hey, all you guys have a bike and I don't."

Brian reached over and gave Stevie a gentle push. "You're kidding? Aren't you the kid from the ferry who lost a red bike?"

Stevie tried not to smile. "You know that already."

Brian stopped in the middle of the driveway and made a big thing about scratching his head, pointing at Stevie, and looking totally confused.

Stevie finally grinned. "I was that kid all right."

Brian snapped his finger and smiled back. "I knew there was a reason I went in my barn today and dug out an old bike."

Stevie's eyes lit up. "Where? A bike for me?"

Collette laughed, glad to see Stevie so excited. Brian sure was nice. Nice to all the Murphys. He looked about the same age as Collette, but he acted like a camp counselor or teacher; someone who got paid to be nice to kids.

"We'll have to go over to my house and dust it off some. It's covered with cobwebs," explained Brian.

"I'll go get some cleaning stuff," yelled Stevie, and took off down the drive. "Don't leave without me, guys." He almost rammed into Laura and her wicker basket filled with stuffed animals.

"Laura!" snapped Collette. "You can't ride a bike with those animals. You won't be able to balance."

Laura's smile fell. "But my animals are going on a field trip to Brian's house. I promised them."

"If you get hit by a car, they won't get the doctor here in time to sew you up again, right, Brian?" Jeff laughed.

Collette smiled a little. Jeff thought he was such a funny guy.

Brian took the basket and shot Jeff a disgusted look as he walked past. "Don't even kid about that, Jeff. Give me the animals, Laura," said Brian quietly. "I'll stick them in my backpack and let the cat ride in my basket."

Collette looked as shocked as Jeff. Why was Brian so upset? Everyone knew Jeff was just teasing, the way he always did. Even Laura knew that. She wasn't the least bit upset about Jeff's comment.

"Here are the rags!" shouted Stevie, waving the yellow bits of cloth in the air. "Mommy said we can keep them."

Mrs. Murphy stood, framed in the living room window, waving. She looked happy, glad to know her children had made at least one friend.

Collette took her bike and glanced over at Brian. She hoped he wasn't going to stay mad at Jeff. That would ruin the whole afternoon. After Brian buckled Stevie in a rickety-looking child's seat on the back of his bike, he grinned at Jeff.

"Maybe we better shoot a few hoops at my house, Jeff, to see if you're as good as you *think* you are."

Jeff broke into a smile, nodding his head.

"Best out of five," he yelled as he hopped on his bike and headed down the lane.

"Wait for me at the corner, guys!" Brian called out. "Hang on, Stevie old buddy."

Laura walked her bike down from the garage and hopped on. "Come on, Collette. We're going to do lots of fun things with Brian today. Aren't you glad he found us?"

Collette swung her leg over her bike and pushed off. "I sure am. He's a great island guide."

Collette felt the warm wind tugging at her hair as she bumped down the gravel drive to the lane. Brian was a great tour guide, and the Murphy's first real friend on the island.

Maybe he would introduce them to lots of other kids today when they went into town. That would be great. When Collette started school on Monday she wouldn't be just another touron; she'd be a friend.

Chapter Seven

Collette's heart took a giant leap as she bumped her bike across Brian's wide front lawn. Brian's house was so small, much smaller than their rented house on Chestnut Lane. She felt ashamed for bragging about having a three-story house in Pittsburgh.

Brian's house was a one-story ranch. The front door was in the center, but there were no steps leading to it.

"Hey, some robber took your front steps!" laughed Laura. She laid her bike down and laughed again. "Do you have to jump up to get in your house?"

"Laura!" Collette got off her bike as quickly as she could. "Mind your own business."

Brian got off his bike and unhooked Stevie. "Hey, it's no big deal. My dad was finishing the house and then my parents got divorced."

"Did your dad take them steps with him?" asked Stevie.

Brian laughed and yanked down Stevie's baseball cap. "No. He lives in South Carolina now. My uncle is going to finish the steps when he stops working at the monument." Brian paused. "*If* he gets around to it."

"He should," commented Laura gently. "Your house would look prettier."

"Laura!" Collette took Laura by the arm and started walking. Boy, some people never thought about what they were saying! Brian must think the Murphys were so rude.

Just then a thin, tall woman wearing an orange-and-brown-striped uniform came rushing out from the back of the house.

"Hi, Brian. Hello, children." She fished inside her pocket as she hurried across the yard, pulling out a set of keys. "I'm Mrs. Kepler and you must be the Murphys!"

Brian started introducing her while his mom smiled. She jingled her keys and laughed. "I am running late as usual. Brian, I made a huge pot of chili, so heat it up for lunch. See you all later!"

"See you, Mom." Brian waved his baseball cap until his mom had backed down the drive and out onto the road.

"I like your mom's uniform," said Jeff. "Does she work for the merry-go-round?"

Collette tried not to groan. Her brothers and sisters were asking too many questions. So far Brian hadn't asked *one* question about the Murphys!

"My mom drives the tour bus," explained Brian. "She should be driving by in about twenty minutes. She likes to check up on me."

"Let's go find my bike!" suggested Stevie.

"Look in the barn, Stevie," said Brian. "I'll be right there."

"Hey Brian. I'll meet you around back," Jeff called. He bent down and picked up a basketball, tossing it in the air.

"You have such a huge yard, Brian," Collette said. "And you have a grape arbor. Wow, does your dad, I mean your mom, make jam or pies with the grapes? And look at that tire swing, boy, wait till Laura and Stevie see that. . . ."

Collette cringed, knowing she was talking a mile a minute. She was trying to say as many nice things as she could about Brian's yard. His house was sad-looking. Not because it was so small, but because everything looked half finished. Like Mr. Kepler had had a thousand projects going and then decided to climb down from his ladder, get a divorce, and leave the island for good.

The back of the house looked worse than the front. Huge chips of gray paint were peeling while blue paint had been applied around the windows and doors.

"My dad promised to come back this summer and finish painting," Brian said slowly. "Guess he never got off the tennis courts."

"Is he a . . . a tennis pro?"

Brian shook his head. "No. My dad is allergic to work, that's all. That's why he didn't stay on the island after the divorce. During the season everyone works as many jobs as they can."

"Maybe you'll drive the tour bus when you get older," Collette said. Brian would look great in the uniform. And he had already been a great tour guide for the Murphys.

Brian bent and filled a bucket from the garden hose. "I already work. Most kids over ten try to get a job. Cleaning chicken down at the grill or selling bait to the boats who dock at the marina

. . . hey, Stevie, bring that bike over here!"

Stevie shot out of the barn, pushing a dusty-looking blue two-wheeler. "Brian, I love this bike. It's just my size!"

Collette and Brian looked at each other and smiled. Both Stevie and the bike were dirty and small.

"Petey was four when he learned to ride that bike," Brian laughed.

"Petey?"

Brian's head jerked up and his cheeks seemed to burn red beneath his tan. "My . . . brother."

Collette leaned forward, looking around the yard. "Oh, great, Stevie will love meeting him. Is he . . ."

Brian picked up the bucket and started walking quickly toward Stevie. His eyebrows were drawn together tight.

"Brian?" Collette stood up and hurried to catch up. "Is Petey inside, or . . ."

Brian spun around so fast, the bucket tilted and water sloshed on Collette's tennis shoes.

"He isn't here, OK? And do me a favor and don't mention it. Don't mention Petey, especially in front of my mom."

"Sure, sure . . ." Collette looked at Brian's face,

then away when she saw how angry he was.

He let out a long sigh, then stared down at Collette's shoes. "Sorry about your shoes."

Collette looked down, then took a step back on the drier grass. Why was Brian so mad? Had his dad taken Petey with him when he left? Did each parent get to chose one child . . . like dividing up books and records?

Collette shivered in the hot afternoon sun. Brian must have felt awful when his dad didn't pick him.

"Brian, can we paint this bike red, like my old bike?"

Brian picked up the bucket and poured a little water on Stevie's head. "How about if I just paint you, kid?"

Stevie dropped the bike and started to squeal, holding both hands over his head as he darted back into the barn.

Collette stood and watched a second, then turned and sat down in the grass. It felt odd to know that divorce and broken families happened everywhere. Even on an island as small as Put-in-Bay. Even to somebody as nice as Brian Kepler.

"Hey Collette, get over here," shouted Brian.

Collette got up and hurried over, picking up a rag and chasing Brian and Stevie across the yard.

Within seconds Jeff and Laura joined the race as everyone shrieked and ran around the huge front yard.

Collette gave a loud war cry and ran even faster, glad to be having fun.

Chapter Eight

The next five days in a row Brian came by to collect the Murphy kids. Once he took them biking to look at a fancy ship, which had been converted into a house and beached on the west shore. Another day they all rode out to the horse farm at East Point, eating peanut butter sandwiches and tossing their crusts out for the sea gulls. Collette had had the most fun when they spent two days fishing at the State Park. Each day she'd caught the biggest walleye of them all. Brian had offered to clean them and her mother had offered to cook them. Brian had stayed for dinner both nights, telling everyone at the table that Collette was the best fisherwoman on the island.

Sometimes while he was bicycling with Collette

and the others Brian saw kids he knew. Although he would always wave, he'd continue riding. Sometimes, Collette hoped he would stop and introduce them; but he never did.

Collette smiled at the other kids, trying not to look disappointed. There would be lots of time for Brian to introduce them once school started. Brian said that the kids from the island were great.

Yet, the closer Monday morning came, the more nervous Collette got. She missed Sarah and Marsha. Tomorrow they would be starting Sacred Heart. Would anyone miss her?

"Brian sure is nice," insisted Collette as she helped her mother set the table. "He said the school was filled with great kids. I hope they like us tomorrow."

Her mother set a pitcher of iced tea in the center of the table. "Everyone will like you tomorrow. Relax. You'll make lots of friends."

That night at dinner, Collette could hardly eat a bite.

"Can I eat your hot dog, Collette?" asked Jeff.

"Sure." Collette pushed her plate toward him.

"Collette, you haven't touched your dinner." Her mother put down her fork and studied her. "I hope you're not getting sick."

"Yeah, cause no doctors live on this island," reminded Laura.

Collette took a small bite of her hot dog. She felt fine, except for a sudden case of nerves.

"I just feel so funny starting sixth grade at a new school. I've gone to Sacred Heart since kindergarten. I know everyone . . ."

"You know Brian, Collette. I bet he's in your grade." Jeff leaned forward and started describing the basketball game at Brian's that afternoon.

"And Brian let me ride the blue bike home all by myself," added Stevie. "Brian said I could keep the bike forever."

"What grade *is* Brian in?" asked Collette. Even though they had spent the whole week with him, Collette realized she didn't know very much about him at all.

"You'll find out tomorrow," her mother said as she passed some fruit around. "I bet he's your age, Collette."

"Brian said that I would love my new school," announced Stevie. "He said that he and Petey both had the same kindergarten teacher and she is . . ."

"Stevie," said Collette quickly. "I hope you didn't ask Brian a lot of personal, private, none-of-your-business type questions about Petey."

Stevie blinked and bit his lip. "I didn't say nothing to him like that. Brian called me Petey three or six times. Brian said, 'Here Petey, hold this screwdriver,' and I said, 'I'm Stevie, not Petey' and Brian said, 'Oh yeah' and I said, 'Who's Petey?' and Brian said . . ." Stevie stopped and rolled his eyes up as he thought. "Oh yeah, then Brian just shook his head and said Petey was his little brother, but he isn't here anymore and then . . ."

Collette slid back in her seat. "I *knew* it! Brian's dad must have taken Petey with him when the divorce papers arrived. Mrs. Kepler got Brian, and Mr. Kepler got Petey."

Laura put down her fork, stricken. "That's not fair." She looked around the table. "Which one would I go with if you guys got divorced?"

Stevie took a big gulp of milk and choked. "*Is* you guys getting a divorce?"

"Of course not," Collette and Mrs. Murphy said together.

"And Stevie, don't *ever* mention Petey's name to Brian, OK?" said Collette. "It would make him really sad."

Stevie nodded. "Then he would cry, right, Collette?"

At the word *cry* Collette felt her own eyes sting. No wonder Brian was so nice to all the Murphys, especially Stevie. He must really miss his little brother.

"Well, you kids better get your things ready for the big day tomorrow," Mr. Murphy said cheerfully.

"Brian said that there is a real nice little girl named Amanda in my grade and she has red hair and she rides the ferry to school everyday . . ." Laura stopped to swallow. "Except when the lake freezes all up and then she takes an airplane and if the fog gets too bad she just stays home and makes snowmen all day."

"Your sentence had about a zillion words in it, Laura," Collette said. She gave Laura a little smile to let her know she wasn't mad or anything. Worried was more like it. Laura never stopped at the end of a sentence when she got excited about something.

It would be terrible if the Murphy children made an awful impression at school tomorrow. Since they would only be on the island for a few months, they didn't have enough time to fix a bad first impression.

"There *is* a school on North Bass Island," said

their father. "The teacher flies her own plane over every day."

"Daddy . . . Daddy!" Laura pulled on his sleeve. "You better go buy us a mailbox 'cause I looked all over the yard and we don't have one. Marsha said she would write me a letter."

Collette pushed back her chair. She wanted to go up and finish her letter to Sarah right now. Wait till Sarah heard about Brian's little brother. He was practically kidnapped from the island. All because of a dumb divorce.

"How come no one wants to write to me?" Stevie dropped his fork.

" 'Cause you're too little to read," Jeff snickered. "Too dumb."

"Actually I did sign us up for a post box number down at the post office," Mr. Murphy explained. "Box 109. It was Mr. Heller's box."

"Doesn't he want letters anymore?" asked Laura.

Her father shook his head. "He died. He's buried in the island cemetery."

Collette shivered, not really sure if she liked the idea of having a dead man's box number.

"Brian said that there are only seventy-five kids

in the whole school," said Jeff. "I mean, that's kindergarten through twelfth grade."

"Wow, that's really small," Collette said. "How many were in the graduating class — three?"

Jeff started to laugh again. "One. One kid named Bill. So for the history of the senior class they had this kid's baby pictures, his baseball pictures . . . it was so cool. Ask Brian to show you his yearbook, Collette."

Collette stood in the doorway, watching everyone laughing. Maybe Put-in-Bay school was *too* small. Maybe it was so small it wouldn't count as a real, legal school. What if Sacred Heart Elementary heard some of the funny stories and said, "Sorry Collette, but we did some special research and checked into the Put-in-Bay school. I'm afraid it just isn't big enough to count. I'm afraid you will have to start sixth grade all over again."

"What if I only have four kids in my class," Collette said. "And two of them are fifth-graders. It doesn't sound like a real sixth-grade class."

"You'll have more than that. The teachers aren't sure of the number until the first day of school."

"Do you think you should write them a letter telling them I'm supposed to be taking extra hard math this year?" asked Collette. "I worked so hard to get into the top group, Mom."

"They'll look at the test scores Sacred Heart sent and know what to do with you." Her father did not sound the least bit worried about Collette's placement in the tiny class.

Collette stood up. "Listen, maybe this school isn't going to work out. Jeff is going to be with third-graders, and that will be terrible because Jeff is already as tall as a fifth-grader, and Stevie will never learn his letters at this rate and . . . and I know that Laura was looking forward to having Sister Lucille."

Everyone in the room was staring at Collette. Her father stopped eating. "Do you want to go home already, Collette?" he asked in a quiet voice. "We just got here."

"I want to stay with you, Dad," said Jeff. He scowled at Collette. "Let's send Collette home to live with Marsha."

Mrs. Murphy stood up and put her arm around Collette's shoulder. "No — we stay together. Collette is nervous, that's all. It's perfectly natural to feel that way. It's been another long day and we are all still tired from the trip. I vote to go upstairs, take your showers, and get ready for bed."

"I vote that Collette should stand in the corner for being her old rude self," declared Jeff with a smirk.

Stevie pointed his new pencil at Collette. "I vote that, too."

Mr. Murphy reached out and pulled Collette next to him. "Leave Collette alone, boys. I realize that tomorrow will be a day of adjusting. There's nothing wrong with feeling a little uneasy about things."

Collette snuggled closer to her dad. "I want to stay on the island so we can be together. But, I just wish they could hire more teachers so . . . so I wouldn't have to share with fifth-graders. I share enough at home. I shouldn't have to share all day in school, too." Collette waited until Laura and the boys raced past.

"I'll be up in a second," Mrs. Murphy called from the kitchen.

Collette bent down and gave her dad a kiss. "See you tomorrow, Daddy."

Tomorrow. Brian had promised to stop by the house for Collette and the other kids on his way to school. As Collette headed up the stairs, she looked out the window in the living room. The moonlight was streaming down through the scraggly branches of the tall, blue pines.

"Make everyone like me tomorrow," she whispered. "Make Put-in-Bay be just like Sacred Heart."

Chapter Nine

Collette ran the brush through her hair one last time, pulling it back over one ear and fastening a navy blue barrette in place.

"Oh that looks awful," she muttered, yanking out the barrette and brushing her hair straight down to her shoulders. She pinched both cheeks and smiled into the mirror. No, too wide, too desperate. She tried another, a smaller, shyer . . . no. Now she looked apologetic for invading the island.

Collette picked up her toothbrush and scrubbed her teeth again.

"You sure look pretty in your new clothes, Collette," said Laura as she squeezed in beside Collette and picked up her toothbrush. "I bet you will get lots of friends today."

Collette rinsed and nodded. She smiled at Laura and retied the red bow in Laura's hair. She was wearing new clothes, too, and looked really cute.

"It's fun not wearing uniforms to school, isn't it, Laura?" laughed Collette. She looked down at her own outfit, smoothing out her skirt and shoving up the sleeves of her beautiful sweater. Her mother had taken them all out shopping last week for new back-to-school outfits. Jeff and Stevie didn't have to wear shirts and ties and Laura and Collette didn't have to wear the plaid Sacred Heart jumper.

"Are you excited, Laura?" asked Collette.

Laura spit out a mouthful of bubbles and nodded. "Yeah, a little. I mean, part of me is real happy and part of me is real jumpy inside, like when I have to get a shot."

Collette yanked at her skirt again. That was exactly how she felt too. Knowing Brian helped a little, but not knowing anyone else made her jumpy. What if the girls on the island already wore makeup in the sixth grade? What if they had boyfriends and talked about stuff in *Seventeen* magazine?

Collette bit her lip and tried not to think too much about it. Life at Sacred Heart Elementary was pretty old-fashioned. Having nuns around kept it that way.

Since she knew her mother would never let her wear makeup in the sixth grade, she reached for the Vaseline and added a layer to her lips. It really looked like lip gloss.

"Did your lips get sunburned from fishing yesterday?" asked Laura.

Collette grinned and shook her head. "No, this stuff just makes my lips soft."

Laura smiled. "Brian must think you're already soft. He told me that you are going to knock the boys in at school."

"I would knock what . . . where?"

Jeff shoved in and grabbed his toothbrush. "He said she would knock them *out*, Laura. Geez, don't you ever get anything right?"

Collette grinned, surprised and happy that Brian had said that.

"Time to go," called their mother from the bottom of the stairs.

Collette hung up her toothbrush and hurriedly tied Laura's ribbon on top of her head for the third time. Laura was dressed in a blue sailor dress with a blue-and-white-striped bow. She looked like a model in a children's fashion show.

"Out of my way," called Jeff as he raced in front of Collette and down the stairs. "If you're tardy at this school, they throw you in the lake!"

Laura laughed right along with Jeff.

Collette held onto the banister on the way down the stairs. She didn't like feeling this nervous, but she couldn't help it. For the first time in her life she was going to be the *new* girl. At Sacred Heart, everyone started out new at the same time — in kindergarten. Except for a few new children, the sixth-graders were the same old kindergarten group.

"Don't forget your new pencils!" said Laura. She held hers in her hand like a bouquet.

"Boy, look at my two girls," Mrs. Murphy said as she handed them each a brown paper bag lunch. "It must be fun getting dressed for school and not having to put on the plaid uniform of Sacred Heart."

Collette smoothed down the front of her new skirt. Uniforms were a little boring, but at least you knew that when you walked into the classroom, everyone would be wearing the same thing and no one would feel awful for being the only one wearing a skirt when the rest were in jeans.

Jeans!

"Mom, what if no one is wearing a skirt to school?" asked Collette. "Maybe I should change into jeans and a sweatshirt."

"You look fine, dear," her mother insisted. "*Very* pretty."

Collette thought of her four uniform skirts, lined up in a row in her closet back in Pittsburgh. They were all brand-new. In sixth grade you switched from the plaid jumper to the more grown-up skirt with oxford shirts.

"Do you want me to walk with you or drive?" her mother asked cheerfully. She bent down and wiped the milk from Stevie's upper lip.

"You can't walk with us, Mom," said Collette. What an instant branding that would be! Mother Goose and her flock of new, strange ducklings, coming up the school walk.

"Why do you have to come at all?" asked Collette. The school was only four blocks down the road.

Mrs. Murphy was at a loss for words. "Well, it is the first day of school, and . . ."

"You can come, Mommy," said Laura, taking her hand.

"Yeah," added Jeff, bumping into Collette with his shoulder. "No one on this island will know it's nerdy to walk with a mom."

Mrs. Murphy looked at Collette and smiled. "I'll get the keys, drop you guys off, and then meet the teachers. After that I will come straight home, OK?"

Collette grinned back at her mother and nodded. Her mom was still young enough to know how embarrassing a parent could be in the wrong setting.

"Isn't Brian coming too?" asked Stevie.

"Not today. Brian called to say he would meet you there. We better hurry."

At the mention of his name, Collette smiled. She should stop being so nervous. After all, she knew Brian Kepler. He was such a nice person he probably had lots of friends. He would introduce Collette to more kids. Pretty soon she would know almost everyone.

By the time they arrived at the school, Collette was feeling much better. It wasn't until they were walking past small groups of students that she tasted the old nervousness. It was as if someone had just turned down the sound. Heads were turning all over the playground to stare at the Murphys.

"Good morning, good morning," their mother was saying, happily nodding her head up and down. She didn't seem to mind that nobody smiled or nodded back. The kids were staring like each Murphy had two heads.

"Why don't them kids say hi back to you, Mommy?" asked Stevie in a loud voice.

"Just shy, I suppose," their mother said easily. She pulled open the front door and walked inside. "Let's go down to the office and say hello."

"Will *they* say hello back?" asked Laura. She was clutching her pencils tightly with one hand and Collette's skirt with the other.

As soon as they met the principal, Mr. Feris, and his secretary, Mrs. Marguard, everyone felt much better. Both made up for the quiet children on the playground with plenty of hellos.

"We are so proud to have you with us," assured Mr. Feris. "Your homerooms are ready and the teachers will make sure you meet everyone. Would you like to say good-bye to your mother now and wait outside with the others?"

Collette started to giggle as everyone took a quick step closer to her mother.

"Can Collette stay in the second grade with me?" asked Laura. "She wants to be upstairs."

Mr. Feris just threw back his head and laughed as though everything about his job amused him. He laughed some more as he led the way upstairs to the kindergarten.

Collette was glad Laura's second-grade teacher gave Laura a hug when she was presented with a yellow pencil.

"Now we go back downstairs for the older children." Mr. Feris spoke in a quiet voice and raised an eyebrow like he had saved the best for last.

Maybe for island schools, being downstairs was a big deal. The opposite of Pittsburgh thinking.

Jeff poked his head inside, smiling when he saw the main bulletin board framed with football cards.

LET'S KICK OFF A GREAT NEW YEAR! announced the paper cheerleader standing in the center of the board.

"Mrs. Marguard, make sure this boy has plenty of recess time!" called Mr. Feris as he headed down the hall.

"And now for Claudette's class," said Mr. Feris. He extended his arm as though he were heading for the very best table in a fancy restaurant.

Collette glanced up at her mother. Surely her

mother would correct Mr. Feris about her name.

"It's Collette, not Claudette," said Mrs. Murphy with a little laugh.

"Sorry," he apologized quickly.

"Oh, don't worry about it. It happens all the time, doesn't it, Collette? It's no big deal."

No big deal?

Collette clamped down her teeth. Today it *was* a big deal! She was walking down the first level of a tiny school, without her uniform or her two closest friends. Now she was without her own name . . . and this was *no big deal*?

"Hello. Welcome to the sixth grade. I'm Karen Wilheim!"

For the first time that morning, Collette smiled without thinking about it first.

Her teacher was so friendly and nice.

"You must be Collette," said Mrs. Wilheim. She stuck out her hand and shook Collette's hand first, as if she were the most important member of the group.

"Hi Mrs. Wilheim. This is my mother, Mrs. Murphy, and this is the principal, Mr. . . ." Collette stopped and covered her mouth with her hand. "Gosh, I guess you know Mr. Feris."

Mrs. Wilheim was so nice she didn't even laugh. "Come on in and get settled before the rest of the group arrives."

Collette waved good-bye to her mother and followed Mrs. Wilheim inside. By the time she was seated, several other children were starting to filter into the room.

Collette sat up straighter, ready to smile and show the new kids she was friendly. As soon as she saw their shorts and jeans, her smile disappeared.

No one was wearing a skirt. No one but the teacher and Collette Murphy.

"Take a seat, children," called out Mrs. Wilheim. She looked over at Collette and smiled again.

Collette smiled back, swallowing and then smiling back in case someone was watching her, wondering if she was going to be friendly or not.

A very pretty girl with smooth black hair slid into a seat beside Collette. She leaned over and poked her red-haired friend with her pencil. Both girls whispered back and forth to each other the whole time Mrs. Wilheim was introducing Collette to the class.

"Collette is from Pittsburgh and will be with us

for the next three months or so. Let's all make her feel welcome," continued Mrs. Wilheim.

Once Mrs. Wilheim started passing out tablets and notebooks, Collette relaxed enough to look around the room. Lots of kids smiled at her. The two girls sitting next to her just stared. The one bent down and rolled the cuff of her jeans, looking right at Collette's skirt while she did it.

"Nice skirt," she said quietly. Then she smirked.

"Thanks," said Collette quickly. She didn't know if this girl was being mean or nice. Collette sat up straighter and turned away. She had a pair of jeans at home. She would wear them tomorrow. Collette looked around the room, wondering why Brian was so late. Most of the seats were already taken, except for two in the back of the room.

Collette smiled. Maybe Brian deliberately came late so he wouldn't have to sit in the front. That sounded like Brian. He wasn't the look-at-me type of kid who wanted to be center stage.

Collette looked slowly around the room, wondering which of the eleven kids were fifth-graders and which were sixth. It was hard to tell. Everyone looked pretty much the same.

"Good morning, Mrs. Wilheim!"

Collette recognized Brian's voice and looked up, smiling at him in the doorway.

"It's *Brian*," the two girls said at once, both starting to laugh.

Brian stayed in the doorway. He handed Mrs. Wilheim a letter. "Note from the office."

"Thanks, Brian," Mrs. Wilheim said.

Collette sat up straighter, giving Brian a little wave. Maybe he hadn't seen her yet.

Brian didn't wave back. He turned to leave, his eyes scanning the room. When he saw Collette, his eyes got larger, then narrowed quickly as though sand had just been blown in them by a sudden gust of wind. He stared at Collette for a moment before turning and walking away.

Chapter Ten

The morning went quickly. Mrs. Wilheim was funny and nice. Nobody bothered to show off or act rude for her. Except for the fact that Collette was the only girl wearing a skirt, it was a good morning.

"Lunchtime," announced Mrs. Wilheim, checking the large clock above the door. "See you all back here in an hour!"

Collette reached inside her desk and pulled out her brown paper bag. She was starving. Lunch would be a perfect time to get to know some of the kids in the room better. The dark-haired girl and her curly-haired friend seemed awfully popular with everyone. But the two of them didn't really act like they needed any more friends. They probably already had too many kids around them.

Mrs. Wilheim turned off the lights and stood by the door as the kids streamed out.

Collette gripped her bag and looked around the room. Oh great, she was the only one holding a lunch bag. Maybe everyone bought lunches at this school. She would have to remember to tell her mom. She didn't want to stick out too much like a new kid.

"Looks like you packed your lunch today."

Collette looked up to see the girl named Melanie smirking at her.

"Yes, I . . . I mean, at Sacred Heart we always . . ." Collette took a deep breath and smiled back. "Could you tell me where the cafeteria is?"

Melanie raised both eyebrows and shrugged her shoulders.

"Looks like it's back at Sacred Heart. *We* don't have a cafeteria!"

She and her friend started to laugh and shake their heads. Melanie looked over her shoulder before they walked out the door.

"Collette?"

Mrs. Wilheim had her hand on the doorknob. "Are you ready? Do you have to meet your brothers and sister to walk home for lunch?"

Collette put her sweater over her lunch bag and nodded her head. Poor Jeff and Laura must be just as embarrassed to be caught holding their bag lunches. Stevie was too young to be worried about anything.

Collette followed the rest of her classmates out the side door. Most of them were already walking away from the school in groups of two and three, laughing and pushing each other.

Stretching her neck, Collette could see Stevie's bright red baseball cap and Jeff's bright red face.

"Man!" Jeff exploded as soon as he saw Collette. His lunch bag had been smashed into the size of a baseball. "I was so embarrassed to be carrying this dumb lunch. Everyone started laughing and saying that I was a touron!"

Laura nodded her head. "Two people said I was a nice touron."

"There aren't *nice* tourons, Laura," explained Jeff. "A touron is a cross between a . . . a tourist and . . . and a moron." Jeff slammed his lunch bag into the trash can and started to walk away. "I hate this place."

Stevie looked down at his lunch, then at the trash can. "Hey Jeff, can I eat the Twinkie in your lunch?"

Collette sighed and pulled Stevie away from the trash. "Come on, Stevie. We better get home and eat and then walk back here."

Laura reached into her bag and pulled out her sandwich. "Stevie, let's eat on the way home and then we can clean out the birdbath when we would be eating, OK?"

"Yeah, and then we can throw our bread crusts all around the yard for a bird picnic." Stevie reached in and stopped to unwrap a sandwich.

"For pete's sake, would you two keep moving?" Collette looked quickly around to see if half the school was watching the Murphy kids doing something else dumb. Something only a touron would do.

Collette saw Brian coming out of the building. He didn't wave until leaving the schoolyard.

"Hi, Brian," shouted Stevie. He held up his sandwich. "You want a bite of my peanut butter and jelly?"

"Stevie!" Collette wrapped her sweater more tightly around her bag and started walking. This whole lunch business was so embarrassing. Brian would probably have a good laugh over it. If he was in the mood to laugh this afternoon. Boy, he was a moody person. Friendly one minute, unfriendly the next. Kids from Pittsburgh were much easier to understand.

"Hey Collette, Jeff, wait up!" called Brian.

Collette could hear Stevie, Laura, and Brian laughing behind her.

"Laura, give me half that cookie and I'll let you feed my cat after school," Brian promised.

Jeff slowed down a little, but Collette kept walking. She could have used a smile and laugh from Brian hours ago when she was a nervous wreck. She didn't need his cheerfulness now.

She needed to go home and write Sarah a letter, telling her how strange this little school really was. No cafeteria! What did they do in the winter when the snow was four feet deep — rent a dog sled and plow through the drifts to get a quick cheese sandwich?

"Hey, Collette!" Brian reached out and pulled on her arm. He was smiling, but breathless. "You sure can travel, lady."

Collette raised her chin an inch and tried to look as bored as Brian had this morning. "I was in a hurry to get home to write my *friends* a letter." Collette turned and started to walk even faster.

Brian laughed behind Collette. It wasn't a mean laugh, more like the kind you give when someone surprises you with something really funny.

"Brian, which homeroom are you in?" asked Jeff. "I was looking everywhere for you."

"I'm in with the seventh- and eighth-graders down by the library," explained Brian. "Which is why . . . well, why I won't be seeing too much of you guys in school. Seventh-graders don't talk to anyone but other seventh- and eighth-graders. But we'll see a lot of each other out of school."

Collette strained to catch every word.

"I can see you at lunchtime," Stevie said. "I'll share my sandwich with you every day when we walk home."

"Gosh, Stevie, don't you know anything?" asked Jeff. "We look like geeks carrying these bags. We won't bring our lunch tomorrow, now that we know you're not supposed to."

"Sorry, guys, I didn't even think to tell you we don't have a cafeteria. I guess I would look dumb at Sacred Heart, walking outside at lunchtime to get a bus and go home."

Laura handed Brian a Twinkie. "You can have this, Brian. Since you don't get to talk to anyone at school."

Collette groaned. There was something wrong with her family. Nobody ever caught onto things.

"Oh, I can talk to people, Laura. But, you see . . ." Brian stopped.

Collette stopped, too, pretending to brush threads from her skirt. Come on, Brian, tell us why you won't talk or see us much in school. Even though you know you're the only one we know in the whole place, she said to herself.

"It's the custom for the seventh- and eighth-graders to stick together. Kind of a private middle-school thing. It's like a club," Brian explained.

"I'm in the Ranger Rick Club," Stevie said. "I get a magazine. Hey . . . how will I get that magazine up here?"

Collette turned slowly and studied Brian's face. The whole idea of a seventh- and-eighth-grade, one-room middle school was stupid. And the fact that they didn't talk to the other kids was even *more* stupid.

"So how do you 'middle-school students' communicate with the rest of the school, Brian?" Collette was glad her voice was so cool.

Brian grinned. "We don't. Not unless we have to."

Jeff looked from Collette to Brian. He looked pretty confused. "What do you mean, you can't say hi to us in school?"

Brian stopped grinning. He looked a little uncomfortable.

"But you'll talk to me, right, Brian?" asked Stevie. "Cause we're buddies."

"Don't count on it," snapped Collette as she turned away.

"Collette, wait." Brian took a few quick steps to catch up. "Don't go making a big deal of this. It's . . . it's just a . . . custom that's been going on for years."

"Well, I think it's dumb," said Collette quietly. Her voice was getting tight as she tried to choose her words carefully.

"But you can still be our friend *after* school, right Brian?" asked Jeff.

"Sure, same as before. In fact, wait till I show you the underground caves. Want to go after school?"

Everyone brightened. Collette scowled at them all. Boy were they easy to please! Sure, Brian, ignore us in school and walk right past when we say hello, but we will be best buddies with you after school when none of your *real* friends can see you.

Collette felt a small stab in her heart. Brian was ashamed to be seen with the Murphys in public.

No wonder he wanted to show them some dark underground cave. The Murphys weren't good enough to pal around with in the sunshine.

"So, do you want to come, Collette?" asked Brian. "I can stop by at three-fifteen."

"No." With a quick turn she marched, then ran the rest of the way to Chestnut Lane. She was glad no one tried to follow her. Glad no one called out her name.

If Brian was going to ignore her at school, he wouldn't get one bit of her attention after school.

Chapter Eleven

In the afternoon the classroom got so hot, Mrs. Wilheim suggested they have science outside.

"You can be in our group if you want," offered Melanie. She scooted over on the bench and made room for Collette. "I hate science, don't you?"

Collette started to say no, she loved it, but she just nodded her head instead. She wasn't about to volunteer any more differences. She already felt too much like an outsider.

"Class, I want you to take your science sheet and try and find as many examples as you can of each category," explained Mrs. Wilheim. She squinted up against the sun. "We have another good hour left so let's get busy. Put your sheets on my desk when the bell rings and then you are free to leave."

Collette leaned over and studied Melanie's sheet. Having science outside was fun.

"I'm Courtney," whispered the curly-haired girl.

"Hi." Collette smiled back.

"I saw your brother walking home with Brian," said Melanie. She stopped, and Courtney and she both giggled. "I saw you running off. Don't tell me Kepler did something disgusting."

"Which wouldn't surprise us," Courtney added in a low voice.

Collette felt her cheeks grow warm. She didn't think anyone was watching at lunchtime. She thought back, wondering how silly she must have looked, running down the street with a broken-hearted look on her face. Melanie and Courtney were probably both behind a tree, laughing and thinking Collette Murphy was the biggest touron to ever hit the island.

"I just had to get home to write my best friend a letter," explained Collette.

"Melanie is my best friend and I am her best friend," announced Courtney.

Melanie gave Courtney a slight frown.

"I said you were *one* of my best friends, Courtney," corrected Melanie.

Courtney didn't look the least bit hurt. She just nodded as if Melanie were exactly right.

"Melanie has *lots* of girls who would love to be her best friend, Collette," confided Courtney. "And not just because her parents own almost everything in town." Courtney giggled. "Although it is fun to be able to ride all day on Melanie's carousel and never have to buy a ticket."

Collette looked again at Melanie. She owned the whole merry-go-round? It was a beautiful carousel, with huge wooden horses, roosters, and pigs.

Melanie shrugged as if it were nothing. "Daddy ordered it for me when I was born. They had to send it clear across the United States."

"It's so pretty. Stevie likes the rooster the best and Laura always wants the white horse . . ." Collette's voice trailed to a halt. She didn't want Melanie thinking she wanted to be her friend just so she could get a few free rides. The truth was, *any* friend would feel nice right now. Somebody to talk to . . .

"Brian said that the seventh-graders don't talk to the rest of the school," whispered Collette. "Is that true?"

Melanie and Courtney both nodded, then smiled. "Yeah, but we'll be in middle school next year and then Brian can talk to us."

Courtney fanned herself with the science sheet. "I can hardly wait. He is the cutest boy on the island. Don't you think he is just as handsome as a movie star, Collette?"

"Courtney, be quiet, he's coming outside." Melanie reached out and squeezed Collette's hand. "Look at his muscles. No other seventh-grader has arms like that."

Courtney snorted. "Well, no other seventh-grader works two jobs, Melanie. My dad says it's a shame that Brian was robbed of a childhood when his dad and Petey . . ."

"Shut up!" hissed Melanie. She frowned at Courtney and then jerked her head back toward Collette. "Brian would kill you if he heard you telling . . . telling other people."

Collette watched as Brian walked over to Mrs. Wilheim, handed her an envelope, and then started back. He looked right over at Collette. Neither of them smiled.

"Hi, Brian!" sang out Courtney.

Brian gave a quick nod and then walked back inside.

"A nod is better than nothing," sighed Courtney. "I am going to tell my dad to ask Brian to come over and chop wood this fall. Lots of wood. I'll stack it and the two of us can warm up over some hot chocolate."

Melanie grunted. "Dream on, Courtney. Brian is cute, but he is such a . . . snob, sort of. I mean, he has been working for my dad since he was in fifth grade and he still treats me like I'm nobody special."

"Girls, how are you coming on your lists?" Mrs. Wilheim called out. "I'll be over in a minute to check."

"Great," groaned Melanie. "OK, three examples of . . . oh, this is so boring. So anyway, I am going to help my dad on Saturday. We have to take the merry-go-round apart and store each piece. Brian has been helping every year and this year I am going to be the one holding the clipboard." Melanie bit her lip before she burst out laughing. "And I will be holding Brian Kepler's *paycheck*."

Courtney's face went bright red as she leaned closer. "You wouldn't . . ."

Melanie gave a confident, slow smile. "Brian can have his paycheck if I get a kiss."

"What?"

It flew out of Collette's mouth so fast she wasn't sure it had been her.

Melanie and Courtney stared at Collette.

"You can't do that," insisted Collette. She tried to keep her voice light, but she felt like screaming it right in Melanie's face. "That's . . . that's . . ."

"That's smart if you ask me," Courtney finished. She sighed and leaned back against the bench. "I would do almost anything for a kiss from Brian."

Melanie sat up straighter and gave a slight frown. "Well, he isn't really my type, but all the other girls will die when I tell them. Even Alyssa, who thinks she is the prettiest, 'cause Brian kissed her once back in fifth grade."

"Well, that doesn't count anyway because that was before Brian got so stuck up. Before Petey . . ." Courtney stopped and slapped both hands across her mouth.

Melanie stood up from the bench and gave Courtney a disgusted look. "You have got the biggest mouth, Courtney. You will never be my best, best friend at this rate. You couldn't keep a secret if it were tied to your wrist!"

Courtney's tears began to build up. Collette could tell that a bad comment from Melanie really bothered her. "Hey, don't worry about any secrets." Collette lowered her voice. "Brian told me all about Petey and . . ."

Melanie spun around, her eyes huge. "Brian *told* you?"

Collette swallowed. Maybe she had exaggerated a little by saying Brian told her *everything*, but he had mentioned the divorce and it didn't take a genius to put two and two together.

Melanie sank back down on the bench. "I can't believe Brian told you about Petey." She said it softly like it was really a total surprise.

Courtney shrugged. "Well, we have seen Brian with Collette and her brothers and sister all over town for the past week, Melanie. I mean, it's not like they are total — "

"Shut up Courtney," Melanie said in a low, mean voice. "I can't believe he told you about Petey." Then she stood up and handed Collette the science sheet. "Here, you finish it for our group. If you get stuck, go ask Brian Kepler to help you."

Collette and Courtney sat and watched as Melanie burst her way into another group of girls. The girls made room for her and then all bent close to listen to whatever Melanie was saying.

In less than a minute, the entire group of heads rose from the huddle and stared at Collette. Melanie looked sad and wounded. The group looked mad at Collette for whatever she had done to Melanie.

"What did I do?" asked Collette. Her heart was beginning to pound under her sweater so fast it was as if it almost made a noise.

"Nothing," said Courtney shortly. "Melanie does this kind of thing all the time. To remind herself that everyone treats her like some sort of a princess. She probably just went over there and said you were bragging about how much Brian Kepler likes you and now he will never fall in love with Melanie . . . stuff like that."

"Brian doesn't like me," Collette said. She was going to add that he probably would never speak to her for running away from him at lunch. But she really didn't want Courtney to run that news over to Melanie. By the end of school the story would be rearranged into something else.

"Brian *must* like you," Courtney said. She said it simply and with a little smile. "Brian must like you a lot if he told you about Petey. Brian doesn't talk to anyone about Petey."

Collette felt chills down her back. Brian must really miss his little brother. And maybe because Stevie was so much like Petey, Brian thought he had something in common with Collette. Some sort of bond that made it safe to open up to Collette a little.

He was testing her by only letting a fact or two slip out. Waiting to see if she would understand what he must be feeling. Collette felt like crying. She had let Brian down in some way, she just knew it.

"Hey, don't let Melanie bother you," Courtney said softly, patting Collette on the arm. "She'll be your friend tomorrow. She thinks you're pretty, and you have nice clothes, and, besides, if Brian likes you, everyone will."

Collette laughed. She just nodded and didn't tell Courtney what she was really feeling right now. She would be a better friend to Brian if that's what he wanted. If he needed to follow the stupid seventh-grade silence rule, then that was OK. The divorce must bother Brian a lot.

Collette took the sheet from Courtney. She filled out the first two questions without even looking up.

"Boy are you smart," laughed Courtney.

"Not really," Collette answered. *But a lot smarter than I was this afternoon*, she said to herself.

Chapter Twelve

It was Melanie's idea to walk Collette home. "I really want to see where you live, in case Courtney and I want to ride our bikes over and play with you, Collette."

Collette was so happy she couldn't stop smiling. Wait until she told Sarah about how friendly everyone was all of a sudden. And the two most popular girls!

As the three girls walked out the side door of the school, they could see Brian and Jeff chasing Stevie and Laura up and down the side lawn of the church.

"Oh, Brian is going to show us some caves this afternoon," Collette said. She checked both girls' faces to make sure they didn't think she was bragging about it.

But Melanie and Courtney seemed happier than ever.

"Maybe you could both come," offered Collette. "My mom could pack us all an afterschool snack and we could have lots of fun."

Melanie just shrugged. "Brian won't let us come. I think he has just adopted your family for the season. He is such a loner. My father thinks he should go into Cleveland for some medical help."

Collette couldn't help but frown. Brian didn't need any help. He was so much fun, and he was nice to her whole family.

"Hi, Brian!" Collette said it loudly, wearing a big smile so he would know right away that she was finished being mad.

Brian stopped running and looked back. He smiled when he saw Collette and just kind of nodded his head a couple of times toward Melanie and Courtney.

"I heard you were going to take after your mom and be the tour guide for the caves, today, Brian," said Melanie. "Can Courtney and I come . . . if we pay the ticket price?"

Brian grinned. "It's free today."

"I have to ask my mom!" squealed Courtney. She grabbed at Melanie's sweater. "Come on and you can call from my house. Brian, don't you dare leave without us, promise?"

Brian laughed. "Yeah. Meet us outside Heinmann's winery in thirty minutes."

"Thanks Bri," Melanie said sweetly. She gave him a huge smile before she slowly walked away. Halfway down the lane she turned and smiled again.

"Who is that person?" asked Laura. "She has really pretty teeth, doesn't she, Brian?"

Brian picked up Laura and slung her over his shoulder. "She's OK. But I like you better."

"Me next, OK Brian?" begged Stevie.

Collette started to smile. Brian looked back at her and smiled, too. "So you're talking to me again?"

Stevie looked back at Collette and frowned. "No, Collette is mad at you, Brian. She told my mom that you were . . . were bad."

"Stevie!" Collette rushed up and grabbed Stevie's arm. "Don't say another word."

Brian started to laugh. "Stevie, tell me what she said and I'll give you a piggyback ride."

"Brian!" Collette suddenly felt trapped.

Stevie ran up and hid behind Brian's leg, laughing. "Collette said that if you were good, then you would talk to us in school. Then she said . . ."

Collette looked around for something to throw at Stevie; a paper cup, a shoe, anything to make him be quiet.

"Hurry, Stevie," Brian laughed. "Then what?"

"Then Collette started to cry and Mom told us to leave her alone."

Collette stared at the ground, too embarrassed to look at anyone. How could she ever look at Brian after he knew she cared enough to cry if he wouldn't talk to her!

"Laura, you and Stevie be sure and tell your mom we need ten pennies to make wishes in the magic creek in the cave."

"Yahoo!" cried Stevie. "Race you, Laura. Winner gets to hold them pennies."

Collette cleared her throat a couple of times. She knew she should just look up, shrug her shoulders, smile, and say, "So now you know you made me cry. Don't make a big deal out of it."

"Collette, I'm sorry I didn't tell you about our no talking rule . . ." Brian was clearing his throat now. "It's just the way our school works. You know, since it's so little we kind of have to invent ways to make groups . . . separate."

Collette nodded a couple of times. "It's OK." She started walking, staring, as her right, then left foot shot out in front of her.

"You're going to trip if you never look up."

Collette looked up, straight ahead.

"Listen, since I was such a jerk about that stuff, I will take Melanie and Courtney with us, just this once, for my punishment."

Collette giggled.

"And I'm getting more than my share of punishment, believe me. You better watch out with those two girls."

"They *like* you."

Brian grunted. "They hardly know me."

"But they'd like to know you," laughed Collette.

Brian smiled back and shook his head. "Oh. They're OK. I guess. They're like bloodhounds, sometimes. Always wanting to know everything about everyone, just so they can show off what they know."

Collette nodded. "There are kids like that back in Pittsburgh, too."

Brian smiled at Collette. "You're not like that; I'm glad."

Collette was so startled, she took a step backward. Her notebooks flew out of her arms and her pencils scattered all over the grass.

"Oh gosh." Collette stood up quickly, grabbing for pencils and dusting off her folder. She could feel how red her face must be.

Brian handed her another notebook.

"Thanks," Collette mumbled, dreading the grin Brian would give her. Why couldn't she have just said thank you instead of acting like no boy had ever said anything nice to her before? She took a deep breath, willing herself to look up and give a carefree, unembarrassed smile. But Brian was already picking Stevie up, lifting him high over his head as he slowly turned around and around in the yard. Collette listened as they both laughed harder and harder, until she joined in with them. The nicest part of school on the island was when it was over.

Chapter Thirteen

"And then, after my dad bought Harbor's Ice Cream and Bay's Souvenirs, he said, well, why stop here? Why not buy a few fancy clothing and souvenir stores, and part of the marina if we can . . ." Melanie took a deep breath and sighed. "It is kind of embarrassing to almost own the whole town if you want to know the truth."

Stevie stared up into Melanie's face. "Do you own the whole lake?"

Melanie glared at Stevie. "Of course not. The lake isn't for sale, Stevie."

"Another few feet," Brian called out. "We're almost there!"

"I think that's wonderful, Melanie," said Collette fairly. She was trying to keep the whole group happy since she was practically the hostess.

"So what does your father do anyway?" asked Melanie. She stopped to brush off her white linen shorts.

"He's a lawyer," answered Jeff. "He has a case in Port Clinton."

Courtney looked interested. "Does he help any famous people get divorced?"

Collette shook her head. "He just helps big corporations with things. Like if bricks fall off a museum, he'll try to convince a jury that it wasn't the museum's fault."

"Okay, we're here," Brian called, getting off his bicycle.

"What does your daddy do, Brian?" asked Laura. She slipped her hand in his and smiled up at him.

"Not much," said Brian shortly. "Hey, here's the entrance. Who wants to go down first?"

"I will," Jeff said. "Wow, are these steps steep!"

"It's the only way to get to the bottom of the cave, Jeff," laughed Courtney. "Commodore Perry hid his supplies and prisoners here."

"Are they still here?" asked Stevie.

"No . . . be careful," Brian called out. "Jeff, duck

your head once you get down there. Stalactites and stalagmites are everywhere!"

"Hey, who turned on the lights?" asked Laura. "I didn't know caves had light bulbs."

Melanie sniffed. "You can't send tourists down here unless you let them see it. Too bad my dad didn't buy this cave."

Brian reached over and pulled on Collette's arm, making a face behind Melanie's back.

"We've been to the island twice before, but Daddy would never let us come down inside the cave," Laura said. "He said Stevie would run off and get lost."

"I would not!" insisted Stevie "*You* would get losted, Laura."

Courtney bent down and pointed to a stumpy stalagmite growing up from the cool damp floor of the cave.

"See that, Stevie. A couple of years ago some kids snuck in here and broke a lot of the stalactites and stalagmites off with baseball bats!"

"Will it grow big again?" asked Stevie.

"Yeah," snorted Melanie. "In another couple of thousand years." She looked over at Brian and smiled. "No offense to anyone *here*, but the police are pretty sure it was a bunch of tourons!"

Collette looked away, suddenly feeling guilty. Tourons were probably blamed for just about everything that went wrong on the island.

Courtney walked beside Collette and smiled. "They don't know *who* did it, Collette," she whispered.

"Oh, the wishing stream," laughed Melanie. "Brian, do you have a penny so I can make a wish?"

"No."

"Yes, you do, Brian," reminded Laura. "Remember?"

Brian gave a slight frown and handed Melanie a penny. Everyone watched as she closed her eyes and tossed the penny into the clear stream trickling under a large overhang.

"I bet I know what you wished for," giggled Courtney. She looked right over at Brian and raised both eyebrows.

Brian turned and pointed his flashlight at a dark corner. "Commodore Perry slept over there, near the stream, and the prisoners were kept chained over here."

Collette shuddered, hating to think of anyone

being kept down here. "Can we go up now?" she asked.

Melanie laughed. "I guess they don't have caves like this in Pittsburgh, do they Collette? Brian and I have been coming here since we were kids, right Bri?"

"Watch your heads on the way up," Brian called back over his shoulder.

"Brian, since it's still so hot, can we ride our bikes down to the monument and swim?" asked Laura.

"The *monument*?" squealed Melanie. "Oh my gosh, that's right. I guess that's where tourists do swim. Uck . . . it's so . . . so public!"

Jeff glared right into Melanie's face. "Yeah, most lakes are public, Melanie. Where do you swim, in a rubber pool in the backyard?"

Melanie frowned as Courtney and Brian started to laugh. She scooped a handful of dark hair off her neck and sighed.

"Actually, Jeff, my family swims at the Crew's Nest." She paused for a few seconds before she added, "It's private."

Of course, Collette thought.

When they reached the top of the steep stone

steps, Brian turned and grinned at Collette. "I'll race you to the monument, and if I win you have to clean the fish I caught last night, OK?"

Collette shuddered. "No way, Brian. If I have to clean fish, I like it in clean squares coming out of a box from the freezer."

"Fish sticks!" cried Stevie. "Let's go eat some."

Melanie and Courtney raced forward and picked up their bikes from the grass.

"*I'll* race you, Brian," shouted Melanie, one leg already across her Schwinn. "And if I win, then my wish gets to come true, promise?"

Courtney threw back her head and laughed. "And I get to watch!"

Brian scowled up his face for a second, then gave a bright smile and nodded his head.

"Sure thing, Melanie. On your mark, get set . . ." Both girls were flying down the lane before Brian got to "go."

Stevie ran over and picked up his little bike. "Hurry up guys. We got to beat them."

Brian just stood, crossing his large tanned arms and smiling as Melanie and Courtney disappeared out of sight. "Don't worry, Stevie. I know a short-cut."

"To the monument?" asked Collette. She hoped

Melanie wouldn't be too mad at her for getting there first.

Brian picked up his bike and laughed. "No, to my house. We'll go check on my cat and then play some baseball. I don't feel like going to the monument today."

"Me, neither," snorted Jeff. "Too . . . *public.*"

Brian raised a thumbs-up sign to Jeff and turned back to Collette. "I'll show you how to clean a fish in case you ever lose a bet to me."

Collette stuck out her tongue and shuddered again.

"Seriously, Collette, forget about the monument. Melanie will get over it. I've been running away from her for years. She expects it."

Collette smiled, then shook her head. It didn't seem like a good idea to get someone as popular as Melanie Adams mad at you.

"I don't want to hurt her feelings," began Collette. "Melanie was so excited about coming with us."

Brian just laughed. "I'll talk to her tomorrow. She can yell at me if she wants. Besides, I want to show you something back at my house."

"Did Mertze have her kittens already?" Collette asked. She would love to see them.

Brian shook his head. "Not yet. This is something I wrote a couple of months ago. It's . . . it's kind of private."

Collette nodded her head, not even trusting herself to smile. She wanted Brian to know that she could be trusted with anything, no matter how private.

Chapter Fourteen

Brian stopped inside the cool barn and helped everyone line their bikes up in the empty horse stalls.

"We can pretend our bikes are little horses," said Laura. She picked up a dusty towel and slung it across her seat like a saddle.

"Come on Laura, let's go find some hay for our horses," suggested Stevie. He patted his little bike. "I'll be right back, Trigger."

Collette looked up above at the thick wooden rafters. It was such a huge barn, five times bigger than Brian's house.

"Did you ever have horses, Brian?" asked Jeff.

Brian shook his head. "No, but my dad bought this place because he wanted to turn this barn into a huge house for us. Pete — I was going to have a huge loft bedroom overlooking the lake, and look, see those boulders?" Brian pointed to a pile of stones in the far corner. "We started to build a fireplace."

Collette smiled. She could just imagine how beautiful the house could be.

"Too bad," said Jeff. He glanced over at Collette.

"No problem," said Brian. Collette could tell he didn't feel the least bit sorry for himself. "I figure I'll start building it myself in another year or two. Maybe you guys can come back and be part of the construction crew."

Jeff's eyes grew large. "I'd like that, Brian."

"You can come up and stay with me for two weeks." He turned and grinned at Collette. "You can stay with Melanie, I guess."

"Melanie!" Collette's hand flew to her cheek. She still felt guilty about ditching her. Melanie was going to be furious tomorrow. She had been down at the monument for over forty minutes by now, probably organizing an "I hate Collette Murphy" club.

"Brian, maybe I better ride down to the monument and get Melanie and Courtney now.

I can tell them we changed our minds and . . ."

"I didn't change my mind," Brian said simply. "I don't want those two at my house."

Collette couldn't tell if Brian was mad or kidding again. "Why?"

Brian kicked his shoe against one of the large gray stones. "All they do is stare and giggle. And Melanie isn't very nice!"

"They like you," Collette said quickly.

"Ha — " Brian shook his head. "Is that what they call it?"

Collette closed her mouth, not sure what he meant. Lots of girls at school liked Brian.

"Brian, why don't we get started now?" asked Jeff. He walked over and kicked the stones. "Why couldn't we start the fireplace? Do you know how?"

Brian shrugged. "Sure. My uncle built his new fireplace last summer. Just takes time."

"We have a few months," Jeff said seriously.

"Well . . ." Brian walked around, looking at the stones. "I could check with my uncle and see what supplies he has left. . . . We could do some of it and then let Uncle Jake finish it."

Jeff went over and started moving some boards

from the stones. "Let's see what we have . . ."

Collette shook her head. How could Jeff help build a fireplace? He didn't even make his own bed.

"Collette, come inside and help me get something cold for the construction crew," laughed Brian.

Back out of the barn, Collette started worrying about Melanie. But she could tell Brian didn't like her. It had been Brian's idea for the trick, not hers.

The inside of Brian's house was tiny, but clean and neat. The kitchen had a little drop-leaf table with two chairs and a blue-checked cloth. Collette looked around, wondering if they had another chair for Petey's visits. Even divorced parents had to share kids on vacations and holidays. Petey would probably be coming for Christmas. For the first time Collette hoped the trial would run over so the Murphys could stay for Christmas. Then they could meet Petey.

Brian filled a thermos with iced tea and pulled a stack of paper cups from the cabinet. "You hungry?" he asked.

Collette shook her head. She didn't think the Murphys should come over everyday and eat the Keplers' food. The other day Collette had seen a coupon book of food stamps on the counter. The Murphys could eat at home.

"What did you want to show me?" asked Collette.

Brian looked worried for a moment, then relaxed. "Well, I said that so you would come back with us instead of going with Melanie and Courtney."

"Oh." Collette didn't even try to hide her disappointment. Not after she had gotten so excited and worked herself up to be a trusted friend with anything Brian wanted to share with her.

"Well, I do have something but . . ."

Collette looked up and smiled. Brian grinned back as he set the tray on the table.

"But listen, don't read it in front of me, and don't tell me if you like it or not."

Collette didn't understand. "Why do you want me to read it, then? What *is* it, anyway?"

Brian held up his hand, and then walked through the kitchen and into his bedroom. When he came back he had a folded square of paper. "I'll take the drinks out and you can read it and then . . . well, maybe you can tell me what you think later."

The screen door slammed behind Brian, and

Collette sank down onto the cool vinyl kitchen chair. She slowly unfolded the paper and started to read:

PETEY

Even though you're no longer here,
I can still hear your step and
the scrape of your chair.
I can still remember everything,
and it just isn't fair!

Collette blinked and reread it again. The poem rhymed and the lines had a nice beat. But it was just so sad. It made it sound as if Petey was never coming back to Put-in-Bay. Like Brian would never see him again.

Collette carefully refolded the note and slid it into her pocket. She could probably help Brian fix up his poem, change the ending so it wasn't so sad. Collette drummed her fingers on the counter and tried to think. "How about . . . I can still hear your step and the scrape of your chair, and . . . and your coming home makes . . . makes life a lot more fair. . . ." Collette looked on the counter for a pencil. Brian did ask for her to read it. Maybe he was hoping Collette could give him a better ending.

Collette heard several happy screams coming from out back. She peered out over the kitchen sink as Jeff raced by, followed by Brian carrying a red bucket, water splashing out in all directions.

Collette laughed and raced out the back door, knowing she could surprise them all with the garden hose as they ran past again.

Chapter Fifteen

"So what did you and Brian do after you dumped us?" asked Melanie. She stared straight through Collette.

Melanie and Courtney had been waiting at the corner two blocks from school this morning, both looking wounded as Brian broke away from the Murphys and raced across the yard and into the school lot.

"Melanie, I didn't know Brian was planning that" — Collette searched for the best way to put it — "that little joke about the monument. He thought you and Courtney would finally realize we weren't coming and then go back to his house. I'm really sorry."

Courtney's eyes popped open. "You went to

Brian's house? You mean, you were inside it? Did you see his room, does he have pictures, or trophies around?"

Melanie interrupted. "Gee, I guess that's, well . . . Pittsburgh humor, Collette. Don't you think so, Courtney?" Her voice was sugary-sweet. Too sweet.

Courtney giggled.

Melanie silenced her with a look. She shifted her books from her right arm to her left. "Excuse me, I see Ellen over there. It will be so nice to talk to someone who is . . ." Melanie smiled at Collette. "One of us!"

"Melanie . . ." Courtney's face turned beet red.

"Well, it's true, Courtney," Melanie replied. "There is a reason that the name *touron* is used. If you're not *from* the island, then you're a *tourist*."

Collette opened her mouth, trying to breathe a little easier. Her whole throat felt tight.

"It was Brian's idea," reminded Courtney. She looked at Collette and gave a weak smile.

Melanie raked her hand through her long dark hair. "Oh, it was *Brian*'s idea! I don't suppose Collette wanted to catch the cutest boy here, did she? No, of course not!"

Collette shifted her own books, embarrassed. Why was everyone letting Melanie act like some sort of ruler?

With a final flounce, Melanie raced across the green grass, flagging down a small group and quickly becoming the center of it.

"Don't mind Melanie, Collette," began Courtney in a rushed voice. "She's just . . . well, just kind of . . ."

"Mad?" offered Collette.

Courtney broke into a shy grin, nodding her head. "Jealous probably too. It isn't all Melanie's fault. Everyone has always treated her like some sort of a little princess since she is so pretty and rich. And she's liked Brian for a long time and now he's choosing *your* family to become close to."

Collette watched as Jeff and Stevie went inside the school building. Laura was waiting under the huge tree in front.

"I better walk Laura in . . ."

Courtney reached out and took Collette's arm. "I like your family. I bet the whole island does."

Collette shook her head. "No, not really. My mom tries to make friends but everyone just treats her like . . . like a tourist." She cleared her throat and tried a brave smile. "I guess tourists aren't really needed on the island once the season ends."

Shaking free her arm, Collette walked quickly toward her little sister. She wished she could just hug Laura tight and protect her from any island meanness that might splash up on her. It would be so great to get back to Pittsburgh, to know that you belonged someplace.

"Hey, Collette . . ." Brian left his group near the basketball hoop and ran over.

Surprised, Collette looked up, taking Laura's hand in hers and giving it a tight squeeze. What did Brian want now? This was school property and he wasn't supposed to talk to her. Now, for the first time, she almost wished that he wouldn't. Melanie and her friends were all staring, watching Brian break a sacred seventh-grade rule.

"Hey, I almost forgot. Mertze was acting real strange this morning. My mom thinks she may be in labor."

"Wow, how soon will she have the kittens?" asked Collette.

Brian shrugged. "I don't know. This is my first time with this kind of stuff. Do you want to come back with me at lunch and check? My mom is helping pack up the train at the amusement park so she won't be able to get away."

"Can I bring her some cupcakes?" asked Laura.

Brian laughed. "Sure, or maybe some newspaper. We can rip it up for a little crib for the kittens."

The morning bell rang and the few remaining groups started to file into the school. When Collette looked up, she saw that Melanie and her friends were the only ones still standing stock-still by the swings. They were all watching Collette and Brian.

"Meet me here at noon," shouted Brian as he bolted across the playground.

"OK," said Collette softly. It was such a faint reply that Laura looked up, squinting against the morning sun.

"Are you all right, Collette?"

Collette nodded, pulling Laura closer to the front door, leading her past the angry girls near the swing set.

"Come on, Laura. Everything's going to be just fine."

"We sure are having fun up here, right, Collette?" laughed Laura.

"Right," whispered Collette. This time her voice was even lower.

She was tired of trying to understand island friendship rules. You had to be an islander before they made any sense at all.

Chapter Sixteen

"It's time to start rehearsals for our Harvest Dinner celebration," Mrs. Wilheim explained. "The seventh- and eighth-graders have written the skits, as usual . . ." Mrs. Wilheim smiled as the class groaned. "And I'm sure that it will be just as funny and great as last year's production," she laughed.

A boy named Bill raised his hand. "Are we still in charge of scenery? My dad has been saving lumber, and I have two jars filled with nails."

"We should make a list today of everything we are going to need," said Mrs. Wilheim.

Collette looked over and smiled at Courtney. Sacred Heart had a Christmas play every year and knowing she would miss it had bothered Collette.

Wait until she wrote Sarah about the Harvest Celebration.

Collette felt the folded square paper in her pocket. It was Brian's poem about Petey. She wanted to give it back to him today. She hadn't mentioned it to Brian yet, other than to say that it was good.

It *was* good, but it was so sad. Too sad if you really thought about it. All Brian needed to do was to add another last line, something to show that things would get better and happier when Petey came back to visit. Then things would seem as if they had never changed.

Collette smiled again. She was happy. Even with Melanie acting so angry, it didn't bother her too much. That was one advantage of not knowing the island kids better. When they started ignoring you, it didn't hurt quite as much.

"My mother wants every parent who is interested in sewing costumes to come to our house tomorrow at ten." Melanie stood up and smiled at the class. "My mom will have coffee and doughnuts."

Collette raised her hand. "My mother is a really good artist. She could draw sketches of costumes, or maybe the scenery . . ."

Melanie turned and crossed her arms. "This is an island event, Collette."

Mrs. Wilheim was across the room in an instant. "Melanie Adams, I am ashamed of you. What a terrible thing to say to our guest."

Melanie smiled smugly. "But she is a *guest*, Mrs. Wilheim. You just said it yourself. I thought the Harvest Celebration was a chance for us 'poor little islanders' to give thanks for making it through another season with the tourons!"

A few kids started to laugh. Collette looked over at Courtney. Courtney was looking at her fingernails.

Collette sighed as Mrs. Wilheim lectured the class on manners and feelings. Collette glared at Melanie. No wonder Brian didn't like her.

"Collette?"

Collette could tell by the puzzled look on Mrs. Wilheim's face that she had been trying to get her attention.

"Yes?"

"Would your mother like to sketch two large pumpkins with a cornstalk or a scarecrow? We could use them on either side of the stage down at Town Hall."

"I could help paint them," offered Courtney. "With Collette."

Collette looked at Melanie, knowing her reaction would be strong. It was. Melanie slapped one hand down on her desk and shoved the other one up through her hair, giving it a squeeze like she wanted to yank it out. "Give me a break, Courtney," she muttered.

A thin girl with thick black braids reached over and patted her on the back as if Melanie were the victim of some awful crime.

But Mrs. Wilheim just beamed, glad her little speech had worked so quickly. "Great, Courtney. Would anyone else like to help Collette and Courtney with the stage decorations?"

The classroom was quiet; no one even coughed. Collette felt a huge warm spot between her shoulders, creeping up her neck and spreading behind each ear. She didn't need any help from anyone else. Especially people who did only what Melanie Adams put her stamp of approval on.

"Don't worry, Mrs. Wilheim," Courtney spoke up. "Brian Kepler said he would be *glad* to help. He promised me this morning."

Collette's gasp was as loud as Melanie's. Both

girls turned and stared at each other. Collette tried to give a relaxed smile. It was never nice to show off, but Melanie deserved some of her own medicine. Maybe if she tasted how bitter it was, she wouldn't be dishing it out so often.

"He said he has lots of wood in his barn," continued Courtney. "He has a huge junk pile of stuff."

"You mean his house?" asked Melanie. She laughed at her own joke. "Is that the junk pile you mean?"

"Melanie," Mrs. Wilheim said. She glowered at Melanie and then sighed as if teaching were wearing her out.

"Well it's true," sniffed Melanie. "My dad said that . . ."

"Be quiet!" Collette snapped. She said it so quickly and loudly that everyone turned around.

Melanie was the only one in the class who didn't look surprised. She wiggled back in her seat and looked relieved, glad that she had finally got Collette mad enough to join the war.

"I think we have discussed the Harvest Celebration enough for the moment," Mrs. Wilheim said. She turned and started writing on the board, her chalk tapping and squeaking across the smooth green.

Courtney gave Collette a sly grin and waved her little finger at Collette. Collette smiled back, wishing she could run over and ask Courtney why she had decided to declare war in the sixth grade. Collette sighed. Actually it was war in the fifth and sixth grades.

Which meant it was a bigger war, a bigger battle to try and fight against the great Melanie Adams.

Chapter Seventeen

Collette looked up at the large clock above Mrs. Wilheim's desk. Ten-thirty. One more hour until lunch. She wasn't a bit hungry, just worried. She had to get to Brian first and ask him to please help with the scenery. Even if he just stood and watched as Courtney and Collette did all the work.

Collette didn't want Melanie to catch Brian first, telling him that Courtney and Collette had volunteered his services without even asking him first. Collette tapped her pencil and looked again at the clock. Ten thirty-two.

Brian would be mad if he thought Collette was busy making plans with him, just to upset Melanie. Even though Courtney had thought it up, Collette didn't deny it. In fact, she was glad she had a secret weapon to use against powerful Melanie.

Just then the heavy wooden door opened and Stevie's teacher, Mrs. Daly, walked in. She whispered something to Mrs. Wilheim. Then they both looked up, staring straight at Collette.

Collette sat up straighter. Maybe Stevie fell down in gym, or got sick right in the middle of the classroom. He did that sometimes, whenever he got too hot or too excited.

Finally Gert, who volunteered as a school nurse, walked into the room, frowning and huffing like she had just put out a fire. She glanced up and down the aisles until she saw Collette. Then she stuck out a thick finger and jerked it back toward her huge chest. "Come on, Miss Murphy. Looks like we should check your head next!"

Mrs. Wilheim hurried over to Gert, but it was too late. Most of the class were already snickering, especially Melanie.

"Gert, I think we can handle this," began Mrs. Wilheim.

Gert folded her arms and waited for proof that they could. "I volunteer here one day a week, Mrs. Wilheim," Gert began. "One day a week for free medical services so I don't think you should be getting in my way now that I'm about to stop a full-fledged attack of head lice from infesting our school."

"Head lice!" shrieked Melanie. She stood up, both hands covering her head as she moved to the side of the room furthest away from Collette. "Pittsburgh cooties!"

Within seconds, kids were racing to stand next to Melanie, smashing down paper sheets on top of their heads like protective helmets. Courtney and five or six others just stared at Gert, Melanie, and finally Collette.

"I don't have head lice," Collette announced. She knew all about head lice from Sacred Heart last year. It was awful, and anyone could get it. Dirty-haired kids and kids with shiny clean hair. All heads looked great to a louse.

"Your little brother has it, Laura has it, and I'm betting dollars to doughnuts that you and your other brother Jeff have it, too," declared Gert. She tapped her fingers against her clipboard and didn't look the least bit sorry for the Murphy kids.

Gert walked down the aisle, laid her clipboard down with a thwack, and dove into the top of Collette's head. "Every head in the school must now be checked," barked Gert. "All right, four eggs near the left ear, another two or three on top of the head . . ."

Mrs. Wilheim gently pulled Gert's hands away and then lay her own cool hands across Collette's shoulders. "Thank you, Gert."

Gert held both hands up like a surgeon about to snap on gloves. "I'll wash up and then start checking. Every head must . . ."

". . . be checked," finished Mrs. Wilheim. "Class, sit down and start your math page. Collette, honey, come with me and we'll find your brothers and Laura. I bet, well, they are probably upset, too."

"Head lice, cootiehead," hissed Melanie from near the chalkboard.

Collette pulled her sweater from the back of her chair as she followed Mrs. Wilheim out of the room.

"I'll call you, Collette," called out Courtney.

Collette stopped and turned to smile. Courtney was really going out of her way to be nice. It surprised Collette that she was doing all this for her. Courtney was deliberately standing up for Collette, but everyone knew that every time she did it, she was throwing a rock at Melanie.

"Do you want me to walk you kids home?" asked

Mrs. Wilheim. "The secretary could watch the class for a few minutes."

Collette shook her head, but hurried down the hall as she saw Laura, Jeff, and Stevie huddled together like a group of unwanted lepers. Gert stood at attention next to them, clipboard jammed under her arm.

"All the Murphy children have head lice," Gert practically shouted. "I just hope we caught it in time!"

Jeff glared at Gert, then stormed out through the front door.

"I'll call your mother and let her know you're on the way," called Mrs. Wilheim. "I'm afraid you'll have to be checked before you can come back to class."

Collette grabbed Laura's and Stevie's hands and marched past Gert without even saying good-bye.

"I don't want bugs in my head," sobbed Laura, picking up the bottom of her skirt to wipe away the tears.

Stevie reached up and pounded the top of his head. "I'm going to smash them bugs up."

"Make sure you use all that shampoo!" shouted Gert. She was so loud that Collette was sure every opened window caught the message.

"Can I go back to school tomorrow?" asked Laura. "I only finished half of my picture today."

"I hate this school," cried Jeff. He waited till Collette and the others caught up. "That dumb Gert came in and acted like I was hiding dynamite in my head on purpose!"

"That Gert is a mean person, right, Jeff?" asked Stevie. He bent down and grabbed a handful of grass, mixing it into his head.

"What are you doing, Stevie?" cried Collette as she brushed the grass off the top of his head.

"I'm feeding them bugs so they won't eat a hole in my head."

Collette and Jeff both frowned at Stevie, then looked at each other and started to laugh.

"Tell me the joke!" begged Laura.

Collette just smiled and shook her head. Maybe something good would come out of this lice thing after all.

Maybe Mrs. Murphy would be so furious when she heard about rude Gert and the head lice that she would start packing immediately and take everyone back to Pittsburgh where they belonged.

Chapter Eighteen

"I am *not* going back to that school," insisted Collette. She reached up and touched the icy cold foam sitting atop her head. "This stuff is really burning my scalp, Mom. Are you sure it's the right shampoo for" — Collette stopped to shiver at the thought of the sticky eggs attached to her hair strands — "lice."

Her mother sighed and added another squirt to Laura's hair. "Gert wasted no time in running over here with a quart jar of the stuff. I think she was almost glad that you children were the only ones infested."

"I don't like that Gert," announced Stevie. "She told me to take a bath more often."

Mrs. Murphy smiled. "Bathing has nothing to do with head lice."

"Yeah," said Jeff. "Even Collette got them and she's a little too clean."

"One mean boy in my class said I had cooties," sniffed Laura. "He said I had . . . *touron* ticks!"

Mrs. Murphy set the shampoo bottle down with a thump. "If I hear the word *touron* one more time, I am going to scream."

Stevie and Laura gave their mother a horrified look. "I won't, really," she said finally. "I just think it is . . . *unfair* to brand people that way."

Collette reached for a paper towel and dabbed at the tiny stream traveling down her neck. "I heard Gert telling you that a district nurse from Port Clinton has to fly out here tomorrow. I bet they make us pay for her plane fare."

Mrs. Murphy looked out the window and shook her head. "If this fog rolls in any thicker, she won't be able to fly in. An hour ago, the sun was out. The weather up here is crazy."

"Everything on Put-in-Bay is crazy," added Collette.

Mrs. Murphy lifted Laura down from the stool and put Stevie on it. She wrapped a yellow towel around his neck and pinned it.

"Don't worry kids. By tomorrow the children in your school will have forgotten all about the lice."

"It isn't *my* school," protested Collette. "Our real school is Sacred Heart. I wish the other side would quit so Daddy could win the case sooner."

"I'm staying here with Dad," said Jeff. He swatted his towel at Collette. "You just miss Sarah. I bet you even miss Marsha, too. That shows the lice ate right through to your brain and sucked up all your smarts."

Stevie and Laura giggled. Even their mother smiled.

"Thanks a lot, Mom," Collette said.

Mrs. Murphy lifted the bottle of shampoo and toasted Collette. "Honey, I am going to smile or crack up. Take your pick."

The oven buzzer went off, and Jeff raced for the stairs. "Can I wash this junk off my head now?"

"Yes, bring down the towel and your clothes when you're finished," called their mother. "I have to wash every bit of clothing and towels in this house."

"Where?" asked Collette. "This little house doesn't even have a washing machine."

Mrs. Murphy rolled her eyes toward the window. "Gert was nice enough to allow me to use her washing machine and dryer."

Collette smiled. That *was* nice of Gert. For a neighbor, Gert had been pretty rude and gruff so far. At least she was starting to be nicer now.

"Yeah," added Laura. "And Gert is only charging Mommy a dollar a load, right Mommy?"

Her mother laughed when she saw Collette's eyes grow larger in disbelief.

"Not quite that much, but almost."

With one quick hop, Collette was off her chair and standing beside Mrs. Murphy. "Don't pay that woman anything, Mom. I would . . . I would rather walk a mile in this fog than give her money."

"Yeah, she can't take our money," Stevie added. "Gert said I make too much noise."

Mrs. Murphy laughed. "When did she say that, Stevie?"

"This morning. I was singing a song for Brian about those monkeys jumping on the bed and that Gert came to her door. She was in a bathrobe and she said that I should let her sleep."

Laura nodded. "She sounded mad, Mommy. She said that . . . that city people didn't have no manners."

"Any manners," their mother corrected.

"We don't?" asked Stevie.

Collette pulled the towel from around her neck and twisted it. "Boy, I really wanted to tell her . . ."

Mrs. Murphy lifted Stevie down from the stool and reset the oven timer. "Gert is a lonely old woman with too much time on her hands. OK? Tell Jeff to get out of the shower, then you should get in, Collette."

Before Collette started upstairs, she turned. "Mom, it's almost white outside. The fog is getting worse. Will Daddy be able to come home?"

"Sure, he would have called by now. Hurry up and don't use too much hot water. We have two more heads."

"Four," added Collette. "Gert said you and Daddy have to use this shampoo, too. To kill . . . you know."

Mrs. Murphy slumped into the dining room chair. "Are we having fun, yet?"

Collette opened her mouth. Now was the perfect time to talk to her mom about maybe going home a little sooner than they had planned. Sure, she would miss her dad. But he never even got home until seven, and he could still come home to Pittsburgh on weekends.

Collette's eyes burned and her scalp tingled. She couldn't remember feeling so sad and trapped.

Put-in-Bay was a beautiful island in the summer. It was perfect for a ten-day vacation with bike riding and swimming. But the islanders didn't want any more people living there and the Murphys were too big a group to hide.

"Hurry up, Collette," reminded her mother. "The shampoo is only supposed to stay on ten minutes."

"All right." Collette took the stairs two at a time. She could think well under a hot shower. By the time she got out, she would know the exact words to use to convince her mom that it would be better for everyone if they just admitted they bit off more than they could chew and packed and went home.

"Jeff, hurry up!" called Collette as she pounded on the door.

As she leaned against the wall, waiting, Collette thought of another good reason to go home. She wouldn't have to face Melanie again. She was too tired to fight in a stupid war.

"Here, a present for you!" Jeff tossed his rolled-up socks at Collette as he came out of the bathroom.

Collette kicked out both socks and closed the door. She wiped off a circle from the steamed mirror and looked at herself. With the shampoo flattening her hair to a dull brown, she looked awful. Not a bit of her face looked like the happy girl that —

"Collette!" Laura pounded on the door. "It's my turn."

Collette reached in and turned on the shower, pulling her sweatshirt and jeans off.

"In a second, Laura."

"And hurry up too 'cause Melanie and Courtney are coming over to help paint something with you."

Collette grabbed a towel and yanked open the door. "What? I didn't ask them over *today*!"

Laura smiled. "I know, but Melanie just called from school — hey! Your hair is sticking up all over, Collette. Go show Stevie!"

"Laura, tell me what they said!"

Laura's smiled disappeared. "Don't get mad at me, Collette. Melanie said that she was coming over to paint something cause she saw Brian at lunch and he said he was coming over to cut something up with Daddy's saw."

Collette sighed and slammed the door. Brian had seen the jigsaw her father had brought up with him. He had asked if he could borrow it sometime and her dad had said, "Sure, as long as you know how to use it."

"Melanie only wants to come over to be near Brian," whispered Collette. "She still hates me." As Collette rubbed her fingers against her scalp, she smiled. Oh well, at least all three of them would be together and they could talk about the play.

Collette turned off the water, grabbing a towel to squeeze out the water from her hair. She slid one damp arm through her T-shirt and jumped into her underwear and jeans. She wanted to get downstairs before Melanie and Courtney arrived. Now was a perfect time for everyone to make up and become friends. Maybe Melanie realized that Collette hadn't meant to hurt her feelings. Maybe Mrs. Wilheim had another talk about kindness and manners and that's why Melanie had called.

"Mom, do we have any pretzels, or Kool-Aid?"

called Collette from the top of the stairs. "Some friends are coming over."

Collette stood up straighter and rethought what she just said, wondering if friends was the right word to use, after all.

Chapter Nineteen

By the time Collette had helped her mother re-make the beds, Melanie and Courtney were al-ready downstairs.

"Hello, Mrs. Murphy," said Melanie sweetly. "I'm Melanie Adams and this is my *best* friend, Courtney Goldberg."

Mrs. Murphy had both arms filled with sheets and towels so she just smiled and said hello.

"Collette, I'm on my way over to Gert's for the first load. Don't let Stevie or Laura get near that saw. Brian called earlier and said that you wanted him to cut out a pumpkin or something."

"Two pumpkins and a post for the scarecrow," finished Courtney. She smiled at Collette. "I met Brian at lunch and told him all the awful stuff that happened with the . . . the hair and all."

Jeff rushed in the front door and grabbed a bag of pretzels from the table. "Hey, Brian is going to start, Collette. Bring out some drinks, OK?"

"Brian Kepler?" asked Melanie. Her smile grew larger, like a cat with the canary in sight. "Oh — Brian is already here?"

"We saw his bike as we walked in, Melanie," reminded Courtney. "You nearly ripped the pocket off my jacket trying to get my brush out."

Melanie's face grew pink, but she just shrugged and turned to Collette.

"I decided that I won't be mad at you two anymore," she said quickly. "I feel sorry that you have . . . lice and that nobody up here really likes you that much."

"Melanie!" said Courtney, whacking her arm.

"Well, we're her only friends, Courtney. And now that her whole family has lice, lots of people will try to stay away from them."

Collette brushed past Melanie as she went into the kitchen to get drinks. "Well, maybe you better go home if you're scared."

Courtney laughed. "Yeah, and miss out on watching Brian?"

Collette was relieved to hear Melanie laughing, too.

"Did you see how cute he looks in that Notre Dame sweatshirt? Too bad he won't ever get there," Melanie simpered.

"Brian's really smart," Collette answered. "You don't need as much money if you're smart. He could get a scholarship."

Melanie rolled her eyes. "Brian *is* a brain, Collette, but how would you know? Did you sneak into the office and look at his test scores?"

"No, but I read a poem he wrote."

Courtney and Melanie both clutched at Collette's arm at the same time. "Brian Kepler wrote you a poem?"

Courtney slumped into a chair. "Oh I could just die. I could just roll up into a tiny ball and die from pure jealousy."

"He didn't write it to *me*," giggled Collette. She watched as the color drained back into Melanie's face. "He just wrote one and asked me to look at it. I'd told him I read a lot of books so he wanted to know if his poem was any good."

"Is it?" asked Melanie. She wet her lips and wet them again. "Can we see it?"

"Please!" Courtney got down on her knees and walked toward Collette.

"Collette, dry my hair, please!" wailed Stevie from the top of the stairs.

"Wait a minute, Stevie!"

"Come on, Collette. I like to read. I read lots of books," insisted Melanie.

"Yeah," added Courtney. "Poetry is to be shared."

"I don't know," Collette's eyes darted to the pile of papers, chewing gum, and baseball cards that her mother had taken out of everyone's pockets before she stashed the dirty clothes in a pillowcase to take to Gert's.

Brian had never said it was a secret. But he also never said, "Go tell the world about this, Collette. I want publicity."

"I did walk all the way over here to apologize!" Melanie reminded her.

Collette gave a slight frown, not remembering the "I sure am sorry" part of her apology.

"Oh, I don't know. I better ask Brian," Collette began.

Melanie sat down hard on a dining room chair and crossed her arms. "Thanks *so* much for trusting us, Collette. Are you this hard on your friends back in Pittsburgh? All I want to do is read one little, unimportant poem."

"It isn't unimportant. It's about Petey."

Both girls gasped.

"Poor Brian," said Melanie.

"Poor Brian," repeated Courtney in a sad whisper.

"Collette, my hair is wetting me all up!" wailed Stevie. "Can I go outside wet?"

"No, Stevie. Here I come!"

Collette looked outside the dining room window. The fog was already rolling in so fast it looked like snow. In a little while everyone would go home. And if they went home mad, Collette might never have a girlfriend on the island.

"Please!" Melanie actually sounded sincere.

Collette reached into the jumbled pile and pulled out the neatly folded square, opening it carefully.

"Here, but be careful and don't . . ."

"Collette!" shouted Stevie.

Collette let out a sigh and turned and raced up the stairs. Laura was already aiming the hair dryer on her blonde curls and Stevie was shivering in a towel beside her.

"Laura, make sure you are all the way dry before

you go outside. Stevie come with me and get your clothes on," ordered Collette. As she passed the top of the stairs she looked down, watching as Melanie and Courtney stood side by side under the hall light to read Brian's poem.

"Hurry up Stevie, my friends are going to the shed to start cutting pumpkins and I want to help." Collette pulled out a pair of clean jeans and a blue and white sweatshirt.

Downstairs Collette heard the front door slam. "Where are your shoes, Stevie?" Collette stuck her head under the bunk bed and pulled out two red sneakers. Collette helped Stevie find his socks and double-knotted his shoes. The front door slammed again and Collette sighed, wishing she could get down there to make sure everyone was getting along all right.

When Collette had finally dried Stevie's hair she pounded down the stairs with Stevie following behind.

Brian was waiting at the bottom of the stairs, his face so red and angry he looked ready to explode.

"Thanks Collette!" he muttered. "Thanks a lot!"

"What?" Collette felt scared. Why was Brian so mad at her.

"What did I do, Brian?"

"What did you do?" Brian shouted. His fury blasted Collette back against the banister. "I trusted you with this poem and you . . . you sold out just to get Melanie back on your side." Brian held out the paper.

"I did not!" cried Collette. Her hand shook as she tried to take the poem back, tried to take back letting the two girls see it in the first place. "They said they loved to read and that they . . ." Collette stopped to swallow, her eyes filling with tears as she realized how dumb her reason was for showing the poem to Melanie and Courtney.

Maybe Brian was right. Maybe she *did* give them the poem as a peace offering. A gift. She traded a trust with Brian so she would have some friends.

"You make me sick," hissed Brian, his own eyes filling with tears.

"Brian!" Stevie's voice sounded scared. He stepped closer to Collette and held onto her shirt.

"I thought . . . the poem is sad and I thought Melanie and I . . . we could help you add . . ." Collette tried to steady her breathing, but every time she looked into Brian's face she could see how mad he was. "You could add another line to show that Petey was coming back and that . . . that things would be OK again."

Brian was quiet for a long time before he looked up at Collette. The anger was gone, but his face looked as if someone had erased everything except the sadness in his eyes.

"It's a little late for that, Collette," he said quietly. "Petey's dead."

Chapter Twenty

"Dead?" Collette felt as if she had been socked hard in the stomach. Stevie buried his face in Collette's leg, shaking and making a scared little sound.

"Kids at school are always asking me about it. How fast was the car going, why was Petey riding a bike alone, where was I?" Brian stopped and shook his head. "Melanie couldn't *wait* to run outside and tell me she saw the poem. On Monday morning, she'll rearrange the facts so that I wrote her the poem, sharing with her how much I miss . . ."

Brian took a deep breath.

"I'm sorry, Brian," Collette said softly, already knowing it wasn't going to be enough. Her shoulders sagged under all the guilt, the sadness of knowing Petey was never coming back.

"Collette!" Jeff burst through the door, his eyes almost popping from their sockets. "Laura's hurt!"

"What's wrong?" Collette cried.

Courtney rushed up, blood on the front of her jacket. "Laura . . . the saw — oh gosh, she really cut her hand. Melanie is with her, but you better get your mom and the medics and anyone else we can find. It's bad . . . it's . . ." Courtney's lips started wiggling so fast she covered her mouth with both hands.

Brian and Collette collided as they both tried to get through the door.

"What happened?" cried Collette. "Did she trip?"

Jeff grabbed Collette's arm. "She wanted to help so she picked up the saw and . . ."

"The saw!" Brian choked out each word. "I left it plugged in . . . when I ran in here . . . this is all my fault."

The chills running up Collette's arms multiplied as Jeff burst into tears. "I think her hand is about to fall off. You wouldn't believe it — there's so much blood . . ."

Stevie backed away and ran up the stairs, crying

and covering his ears. "Get Mommy! Go help Laura!"

"I'll call the medics," Brian said, rushing into the kitchen.

"I'll get some towels," Courtney said as she raced up the stairs. "Come on, Stevie. Help me find towels."

Collette ran out onto the porch, her eyes straining toward the tiny pinpricks of light coming from the shed. She could hear Laura crying. "Jeff, stay with Stevie. Call Mom at Gert's and tell her to hurry home."

Collette picked up Brian's heavy flashlight from the hall and moved slowly down the walk. The fog was still so thick, she could barely see in front of her.

Collette tripped over a small bush and stumbled slowly toward the dim floodlight outside the shed. Laura's crying from the shed stopped suddenly, but the silence was even scarier, as though the fog had finally swallowed everyone up for good.

Collette heard footsteps behind her and felt Brian's hand on her arm. "Here — I got some towels — Medics are coming. Jeff is calling your mom."

Collette felt the warmth of Brian's fingers beneath her sweatshirt as he steered her quickly across the grass. She started shaking. "She's going to be all right, isn't she, Brian?"

Brian squeezed her arm and kept walking. "The medics are coming," he said quietly. "It's all my fault. I can't believe I left the saw plugged in — how stupid!"

As the shed light grew brighter, Collette broke free from Brian and raced into the shed. Lively music was still playing from a tiny transistor radio hanging from a beam as if nothing terrible had happened.

Collette looked to the left and saw Melanie holding Laura on her lap on the floor. Laura's face was wet with tears, the entire front of her pink jacket and jeans covered with blood.

"Laura!" Collette dropped the flashlight and hurried over, kneeling down, not sure of what to pat or touch. "Mommy's coming, don't worry."

"Watch her hand," Melanie said quickly.

"How bad is it, Mel?" asked Brian. He took the flashlight from Collette and held it closer. "Let me see your hand, Laura."

Melanie bent and kissed Laura's head. "Laura has been so brave. I bet she's going to be great when they fix . . ." Her voice faltered. When she looked up there were tears in her eyes. "She needs a lot of stitches."

Collette bit her lip. Was Laura going to lose her hand?

"I don't want stitches," cried Laura. "I fell down the stairs once and got them and they pinch."

Collette took Laura's good hand and squeezed it. "I'll stay with you, Laura."

"Don't think about the stitches, just think about Mertze and those kittens," added Brian. "Maybe she's having them right now. You've got to get fixed up so you can help me, remember, Laura." Brian knelt down and patted Laura's knee. "You can help me name them. You can name them all."

Laura smiled, then started to cry again. "Where's Mommy? My hand feels like it's on fire."

The sound of a siren outside made Collette jump. She moved closer to Melanie and Laura, patting Laura's hand and leg. "Laura, I think the doctors are here to look at your hand."

Two men walked through the door, huge flashlights and medic bags in hand.

"Well, we made it," said the larger man with a

smile. "Hi, honey, Let's take a look. You tried to use the saw, did you?"

Laura nodded, her eyes getting larger as the man gently took her hand in his and looked carefully. "Jack, she's going to need stitches — *lots* of stitches — she'll need more care than the island has . . ."

"What?" Collette cried. "What does that mean? Can't you *get* stitches here?"

The man smiled at Collette and then at Laura. "Well — I think she's going to need to get off the island. There's a hospital on the mainland. The cut is too deep. Jack, get me a bandage. We better start an I.V. here."

The other man came over and they all formed a huddle, inching Collette out so she was standing on the outside, trying to see what they were doing and trying not to see a thing.

"It hurts," sobbed Laura.

Melanie was still holding Laura and she kept talking to her the whole time, telling her all about the dog she had and how much trouble he gets into and how scared she was when she had to take a ferry in the middle of the night because a big splinter got infected in her foot. . . . Collette smiled at Melanie. She was being so kind. She felt a rush of guilt all over again for deserting her at the monument.

"Think we can wait till morning when the fog lifts, Walt?" Jack asked.

Walt didn't even look up. He kept wrapping Laura's hand and shook his head. "We have to try and get her off the island tonight."

"Laura!"

Collette turned and burst into tears when she saw her mother and Gert standing in the doorway.

"Mommy!" cried Laura. "Look at my hand!"

Collette rushed to her mother, but she just hurried past and broke into the huddle, asking questions and trying to hug Laura.

Collette turned to Gert, standing next to her, a coat thrown over a faded bathrobe and her feet jammed into slippers.

"She'll be fine," Gert promised. She looked at Collette for a minute before she reached out and pulled her close for a hug.

Collette closed her eyes and let the warm tears fall, soaking right into the bumpy, scratchy fabric of Gert's coat.

Laura started to cry again as they lifted her onto the stretcher and started to roll her out into the foggy, dark night.

Gert patted Collette again and again, hushing her and stroking her hair.

Collette pulled away and wiped her face with her sleeve, looking up to see how Brian was doing. He had looked so worried when Melanie had said ". . . lots of stitches."

But when Collette looked up, Brian was gone.

Chapter Twenty-one

Collette rode with her mother and Laura to the medical building next to the elementary school. The jeep inched slowly down the road, the bright lights barely a flicker against the blanket of fog.

"We have to try to get your daughter off the island," explained Jack. He turned slowly into the graveled parking lot in front of a small square building.

"But, why can't you two just stitch her hand here?" Mrs. Murphy's voice was shaking. "It's crucial that stitches be done within a few hours, isn't it?"

Walter opened the back doors and hopped out, reaching back inside for Laura's stretcher.

"I'm comfortable with putting in two or three

stitches from a boating mishap or a baseball injury, but . . ." Jack was talking softly and smiling at Collette and her mother, but you could hear the urgency in his words. "Your daughter's injury is serious. She's going to need a plastic surgeon."

"Well, then let's call someone from the mainland," cried Mrs. Murphy. "Call them right now."

"We're going to try to get help here as soon as possible," Jack said. He walked around the side of the jeep and helped Walt with the stretcher.

Collette shuddered as she followed her mother up the cement stairs to the medical building.

"Trouble is, with this fog, you aren't going to be able to bring anyone in," Gert said matter-of-factly.

Collette gripped Gert's arm. What was she talking about? Of course someone would come. They would hop in their plane the moment they heard a little seven-year-old girl was hurt terribly.

"Why can't we just take the ferry out and go real slow and take Laura into Port Clinton?" asked Collette. "They have a hospital there."

"Island ferries don't have radar. There's no radar on the whole island, honey." Gert squeezed Collette's shoulder. "Once this fog swallows us up, it keeps us prisoners till it moves on."

"But this is an emergency!" cried Collette.

"I know, honey, but this is a bad fog. We're doing what we can."

Collette's hand froze on the doorknob.

Gert reached around her and yanked the door open hard, pushing Collette into the brightly lit room.

The warmth of the room heated Collette's cheeks instantly, but inside she felt frozen. She looked up at Gert, studying her face. Was Gert going to tell her that nobody on the island was going to try and help them get Laura off the island because it was too risky? Or was it because Laura was a Murphy, someone who really didn't belong on the island in the first place?

Collette slid into a metal chair, looking down at her hands instead of at the group gathered around Laura. Jack was getting a shot ready while Walter adjusted his headphone and turned knob after knob on the huge radio filling a table in the corner.

Not even Brian had stayed around to see what was going to happen. Collette felt the tip of her nose tingle, and blinked hard against the tears stinging her eyes. Collette had disappointed Brian, but what had Laura ever done except think he was the greatest?

People always said emergencies drew people together, making them share their last scrap of food with strangers, or rush into a burning building to rescue a little kid.

Collette closed her eyes. She felt alone and sad for herself and her whole family. The fog had trapped them, separating them from help and people who cared about them. They really were outsiders, separated from the islanders by more than fog.

Collette looked up, watching as her mother helped Jack clean and rewrap Laura's hand.

"Your husband can't get a plane back, Mrs. Murphy," called Walt. He adjusted a few dials and took his headphones off. "Fog's too thick. He's at the Port Clinton Hospital now, waiting for word from us."

Collette saw the last bit of color leave her mother's face. But she nodded, then took a deep breath and smiled down at Laura. "Well, won't we have a lot to tell Daddy when we see him?"

"Mommy," cried Laura. "I want to go home now. Just let me go home."

Jack brushed back Laura's hair and smiled. "Hey, little girl. We're trying our best to get you a plane. You can't back out on us now."

Walt turned back to the radio, putting on his headsets and turning knobs.

"Can do . . . yes, sir. We'll be waiting there for you. Thanks, fellas . . . thanks a lot."

Walt pulled off his headset and smiled. "The Coast Guard is sending over their big copter. It has huge floodlights which might just cut through the fog. Come on guys. We have a date at the airport."

Gert stood up, yanking at her jacket and clearing her throat. "I'll go on back to your house and look after your kids. I'll fix them some soup and stay with them till you get back. Don't worry none. I guess I know kids well enough by now."

Mrs. Murphy smiled, then covered her eyes with a trembling hand. Gert reached out and patted Mrs. Murphy on the back. "No telling what kind of trouble that Stevie is in by now." She laughed and winked at Collette. "My youngest was wilder than your Stevie if you can imagine that!"

Everyone laughed and started getting ready to leave. Walt got down an extra blanket and wrapped it around Laura. He handed Mrs. Murphy a bright orange slicker to put on and started turning off lights.

"Where did that Brian go off to anyway?" asked Gert. "I wanted him to walk me home."

"Collette, why don't you go home with Gert," suggested Mrs. Murphy.

Collette shook her head. She wanted to make sure Laura and her mother got off the island. And if they didn't, she wanted to wait with them for help to come.

Gert waved her hand. "I could walk this island with a black sack over my head. I know every square inch of it."

Collette watched Gert walking quickly down the lane, as if she had built in radar beneath her curled hair. As Collette crowded into the backseat, she looked out into the night, wondering where Brian was, why he just left without saying good-bye.

But she already knew why. He probably left because he couldn't stand to be in the same room with Collette Murphy anymore. Maybe he was afraid Collette would just stand up on a chair and recite Brian's poem to the whole room. . . .

Collette sighed. Or maybe the medical building was just an awful reminder of the time Petey was rushed there, hurt and needing help.

"Here we go," called out Jack in a cheerful voice. "Let's see what kind of luck you Irish really do have."

"Too bad we don't have floodlights at the airport," Walt said. "I don't mind not having a real paved runway, but it sure would be nice on nights like this to have a little light from below."

Collette shivered in the backseat. How could a helicopter possibly land? There was no radar to lead it through the thick fog, no lights to guide it down.

Beside her, Collette felt her mother's hand on her arm. They looked at each other and smiled. Laura was finally closing her eyes and sleeping. Walt had given her a shot for the pain, and it was finally letting her rest.

Laura looked so little.

Mrs. Murphy looked down at Laura and shook her head. "This was too close, Collette. With four children, especially with Stevie and the water. . . . I don't know. Maybe we should just go back to Pittsburgh."

Collette nodded. "Maybe we just don't belong up here," she whispered back.

Jack swore as the jeep bumped off along the

shoulder of the road. He pounded the dashboard and jerked to the left, riding along the smooth road once again.

"My brights are like a lightning bug in a closet," he grumbled.

"How much further?" asked Collette. She tried to picture the route in the daytime. In the summer her family would ride bikes after dinner, past the church and school, turning and then cutting past the winery, heading away from town to the airstrip. It had seemed so uncomplicated then.

"Should be right about here, Jack," said Walt, reaching out and pointing out into the whiteness. "Slow down. Stop here and let me look."

Jack stopped and Walt opened his car door, stepping out and almost disappearing into the mist. When his head popped back inside, he was grinning.

"Well now, have we got a surprise for you ladies," Walt slapped Jack on the shoulder and started to laugh. "Head on out, man. Can't you see the airport?"

Collette and her mother both looked at each other, puzzled. What was Walt talking about? All you could see outside was whiteness, like a giant sheet wrapped tight around the jeep.

As the jeep headed down the road, Jack started to laugh. He shoved his baseball cap back from his head and laughed even harder. "Would you look at that?"

Collette leaned forward in her seat, straining to see.

Ahead in the distance she could see tiny bits of light dancing on and off from the center of the fog.

As they got closer, Jack threw back his head and laughed again. Walt stuck his head out the window and gave such a loud hoot that Laura's eyes flew open.

"Let me see those lights!"

The closer the jeep came, the larger and brighter the lights.

"If that copter can't see that fine runway, we're all in trouble," laughed Jack. "Who arranged that so fast?"

"It's a runway," repeated Collette, beginning to smile as she stuck her head out the window next to Walt's. "A real runway of lights. Where did the lights come from?"

The jeep rumbled across the grassy field, getting closer and closer to the flashing bright lights. Finally Collette could make out through the moving waves of fog, car after car, each two feet apart, flashing their lights on and off, on and off.

Brian stood by the first car, waving his lantern up and down like a train conductor. Collette couldn't believe it. It looked like the whole island was out there.

The copter hovered overhead, invisible yet deafening with the blades whipping through layer after layer of fog.

Collette looked over at Brian, wondering why the copter didn't land. What was it waiting for? Surely the lights were bright enough to cut through the fog.

Just as quickly as it had arrived, the copter's blades disappeared.

Collette looked back at the jeep, at her mother's face pressed against the window. She didn't want to have to go back and tell her the helicopter couldn't land.

At first Collette thought she heard her own heartbeat, spinning out of control. She turned her face up to the sky.

It was back, the helicopter was back pulling in from another direction, sounding even more powerful, more determined to split through the fog.

Collette watched as the bottom of the helicopter

lowered itself through the clouds, the blades dark against the fog.

Within seconds Jack and Walt were carrying Laura and steering Mrs. Murphy toward the copter. Before the blades had even slowed, they were all inside and the copter rose again like an impatient eagle.

Collette stood for what seemed forever, staring up at the sky until she couldn't see or hear anything except the silent whiteness.

She didn't hear Brian come up beside her until she felt his heavy sweatshirt around her shoulders.

She watched as the first cars started up their engines and moved slowly off the runway, disappearing as tiny pinpricks of light as they snailed their way back into town.

Collette shivered. Everyone in those cars was a hero. Each person had driven out on a dangerous night to be part of a living runway. She would have to thank them all for doing that. It would take a long time but Collette would find them all and thank them for helping the Murphys when they really needed it.

"Thank you, Brian — thanks so much," said Collette. "How did you manage all this?"

Collette now knew why Brian had left so quickly.

"We did it with . . . with Petey. He got off the island but . . . he died the next day at the hospital."

Collette said, "I'm real sorry about Petey, Brian. If you . . . if you ever want to . . . well, talk or anything. . . ." Collette stopped and took a deep breath. "I do know how to keep a secret, I mean, once I know it's a secret. I am so sorry about showing the poem, Brian."

Brian nodded silently, watching the last car pull onto the road. "It's okay. I guess I should have trusted you with the whole story, Collette. Petey was hit by a car." Brian's mouth clamped down hard. "It was real bad. My dad never did get over it. I know that's why he left the island. Too many memories."

Collette didn't know what to say, so she didn't say anything. Instead she squeezed Brian's hand, hoping he knew how she felt.

"Hey, are you two going to stand there holding hands all night?" hollered Jack from the jeep. "Some of us would like to get some hot coffee, you know."

"Yeah," laughed Brian. "They just want to sit around and talk about the big rescue. You Murphys are part of island history now, whether you like it or not."

"I like it," laughed Collette. "I *love* it!"

Collette and Brian started to run, grabbing on to each other's hands and racing back toward the dim lights of the jeep.

Chapter Twenty-two

Collette was glad the night was so dark on the way home. She wasn't quite sure what she should say to Brian, other than, "Thank you for calling all of your friends and asking them to help us out." She had already said that. Now that she knew the truth about Petey, she felt terrible. Poor Petey. Poor Brian!

She bit the tip of her tongue so she wouldn't start talking too fast and say things she didn't mean. Or worse yet, say in a dumb way what meant the most to her. How could she ever thank Brian enough for helping get Laura to the hospital?

"Your sister is going to be fine," Walt called

back over his shoulder. "The pilot of the copter said the fog is breaking up around Port Clinton. They're going to be there in no time."

Collette nodded, wishing the fog would disappear completely.

"Your sister is a lucky little girl," declared Walt. He ran his fingers through his hair and turned to smile at Collette. "She'll probably need a little therapy, to stretch the muscles again, but she's going to be good as new. She'll be running around the island in a few weeks."

Collette nodded again. Laura was lucky; all of the Murphys were. Lucky to still be all together, with all of their fingers and toes and . . . Collette swallowed hard, knowing the huge tight lump in her throat wasn't going to go away. Why were the Murphys so lucky again when they already had more luck than so many others?

They had already had summers of bike riding under a perfectly blue sky at Put-in-Bay . . . picnics on the smooth glacial rocks jutting out into the lake, trips downtown to listen to the bands and watch the fancy boats docking at the marina.

In the past, the houses they passed were pretty and fun to look at as they raced by on their bikes. Collette sighed, feeling guilty and selfish knowing she had never really thought about the people who lived inside, or the people who handed them cones, or the men who helped them load their bikes onto the crowded ferry.

Some of them had been inside the silent cars lined up at the airport tonight, waiting till Brian gave the signal so they could flash on their headlights.

"You OK, Collette?"

Brian leaned over and tugged on Collette's ponytail.

"Don't look so sad, Collette. Laura is going to be fine. I bet your mom calls as soon as we walk in the house."

Collette nodded, the news too good to hope for. Her father and mother would meet at the hospital, and they would all come home together tomorrow on the ferry.

"I heard your mom say you were heading back to Pittsburgh," said Jack, slowing even more as he turned onto Chestnut Lane. "I bet it will feel good to be back home."

"Yeah, I guess so," stammered Collette. "I mean, I want to go back to Pittsburgh *one* day, but . . . but I like it here." Collette smiled at Brian. "My mom was just real nervous about Laura's hand and everything. My mom loves the island."

Brian jabbed Collette in the arm. "Hey, you guys can't go back to Pittsburgh and leave me with Mertze and her kittens. You promised to help."

Collette smiled, shaking her head. "We'll probably stay. Besides, my mom will want to stay, too after . . . after everyone was so nice. She'll feel better tomorrow when the fog is gone and things are a little less crazy. . . ."

Brian laughed. "Things are not going to get less crazy, Collette. Some of the ladies were talking about dropping hot casseroles and bread off at your house. It's going to get more crazy. Everyone knows people turn on their ovens the moment an islander has an emergency."

"An islander . . ." Collette felt a rush of prickles down her arms. She started to smile, leaning back into the seat. Jack swung the jeep up the gravel drive and stopped.

"Can you come in and . . ." Collette scratched the back of her neck, hoping she was going to say the right thing. "Can you come in and have some pie, I mean, if there is some and . . ."

"Oh, I'm sure Gert has a pot of fresh coffee going and some of her banana bread in the oven already. Sure, I'll call my wife and let her know your sister is OK. Our little Jenny is in Laura's class."

"I'm coming in to make sure Stevie and Jeff are OK," said Brian. "They were really scared."

Collette watched as they got out of the jeep, each laughing and slapping each other on the back like they had all just made it through a blizzard together.

In a way, they had. Everyone had been just great.

As soon as Collette pushed open the door she smelled the coffee and cinnamon buns. Melanie and Courtney looked up and smiled. Everyone was sitting on the floor around the coffee table, playing cards. Stevie was sitting on Melanie's lap, his eyes red and puffy.

"Is Laura OK?" Jeff asked quickly.

"Laura is going to be fine. The helicopter picked her up," said Collette. "Brian organized a great runway."

"That's no surprise," said Melanie. "Brian deserves to be our local island hero."

Collette was glad to see Melanie smiling so nicely at Brian; you could tell that she meant every word she said.

Gert snapped the dish towel from her shoulder and waved everyone inside. "Well, come on in and close the door. No need to let all this foggy night air in."

The phone started to ring and Gert's hands flew up in the air. "If it's not one thing in this house, it's another," she fussed.

Jeff raced to the phone and picked it up. He nodded his head up and down several times, his smile getting bigger and bigger. "OK, I'll tell them. Bye, Mom, I love you."

Jeff hung up the phone. "Mom's at the airport and they're heading out for the hospital now. Two police cars are going to lead them. She says that we can stay up till nine and not to give Gert any trouble."

Gert rolled her eyes and swatted Jeff with a towel. "I'll trouble you one, sonny."

Everyone started laughing and talking at once.

"Where's that coffee, Gert?" asked Walt, heading back to the kitchen. "Are those your famous sticky buns I smell?"

"I'm a-coming, I'm a-coming," huffed Gert, skuffing by in her bedroom slippers. "And don't you think you're going to get more than two sticky buns tonight, Mr. Walter Brich."

As Gert passed Collette and Brian, she reached out and grabbed them both, hugging them tight. "About time you two got home," she said, pulling back and smiling. "I was starting to worry about you."

Collette hugged Gert back, glad Gert cared enough to worry. Glad that everything finally felt like home.